Books by Scott Corbett

The Trick Books

THE LEMONADE TRICK
THE MAILBOX TRICK
THE DISAPPEARING DOG TRICK
THE LIMERICK TRICK
THE BASEBALL TRICK
THE TURNABOUT TRICK
THE HAIRY HORROR TRICK

What Makes It Work?

WHAT MAKES A CAR GO?
WHAT MAKES TV WORK?
WHAT MAKES A LIGHT GO ON?
WHAT MAKES A PLANE FLY?
WHAT MAKES A BOAT FLOAT?

Suspense Stories

MIDSHIPMAN CRUISE
TREE HOUSE ISLAND
DEAD MAN'S LIGHT
CUTLASS ISLAND
DANGER POINT: THE WRECK OF THE BIRKENHEAD
ONE BY SEA
COP'S KID
THE BASEBALL BARGAIN
THE MYSTERY MAN
THE CASE OF THE GONE GOOSE
THE CASE OF THE FUGITIVE FIREBUG
THE CASE OF THE TICKLISH TOOTH

The Case of the Ticklish Tooth

The Case
of the
Ticklish
Tooth

by SCOTT CORBETT

Illustrated by Paul Frame

An Atlantic Monthly Press Book
Little, Brown and Company
BOSTON   TORONTO

LIBRARY OF CONGRESS CATALOG CARD NO: 71–140480

01150   W0871   T03/71

FIRST EDITION

ATLANTIC–LITTLE, BROWN BOOKS
ARE PUBLISHED BY
LITTLE, BROWN AND COMPANY
IN ASSOCIATION WITH
THE ATLANTIC MONTHLY PRESS

Published simultaneously in Canada
by Little, Brown & Company (Canada) Limited

PRINTED IN THE UNITED STATES OF AMERICA

To the Cheerful Pessimist,
Doc Peters
D.D.S.

The Case of the Ticklish Tooth

One

INSPECTOR TEARLE glanced reluctantly at his electric wristwatch. Yes, the time had come. He gritted his teeth —

"Ouch!"

— and ungritted them in a hurry. It was not the moment to be pressing them together, as one of his back teeth had been quick to remind him.

Once again the tooth had sent that zigzag message flashing through Roger's skinny body from head to toe. Not pain, exactly, but sort of a barbed-wire tickle. As he had put it to Dr. Butterick, trying to minimize the whole business, his tooth felt "ticklish."

"I'll bet it does, and it'll be more than that if we don't get in there and dig that tickle out," Doc had replied with that grisly humor dentists so often use to cheer up their patients. That was yesterday at 3 P.M., nearly twenty-five long hours ago.

When he had finished cleaning Roger's teeth, he consulted his appointment book.

"Tell you what, Inspector. I'm pretty well jammed up, but I'd like to fit you in if I can. So if I haven't phoned you by four tomorrow, give me a ring and remind me."

Words of doom, they were. Even now, as he sat at his desk recalling them, Inspector Tearle came dangerously close to regritting his teeth. Because now it was time to climb down out of his office and make the dreaded phone call.

He glanced around him and tried to fight the craven dread in the pit of his stomach by reminding himself who he was. How many established twelve-year-old detectives were there who had an office in a tree house? With a desk, a chair, a telephone, and a two-drawer steel filing cabinet in it, all protected by a secret burglar alarm of his own devising? How many, if there were any others, had cases to their credit of the caliber of the Chadburn Goose Case and the Milford Arson Case,* to name but two? Had not the entire village of East Widmarsh, as a result of his activities, given him the nickname of "Inspector"?

Impressive thoughts, these, but futile. Even as he was thinking them, his tongue strayed cautiously in the direction of that back tooth, probing gently, hoping to find Nobody Home . . .

* See *The Case of the Gone Goose* and *The Case of the Fugitive Firebug.*

4

"Ouch!"

The tickle was still there, still in business. There was no escaping it. Once again he was faced with the grim Novocaine Dilemma. If he refused novocaine, he would have to endure the miseries of the Drill; if he accepted novocaine, he would suffer the horrors of the Needle. And it was going to be a big cavity. He just knew it would be. It was going to feel as if a couple of little men had climbed into the pit with picks and shovels. Groaning, Roger reached for the telephone and put in a twenty-five-foot phone call.

A bright voice answered him impatiently.

"Oh, Roger, what is it now? Are you trying to ruin my brownies?"

Hardly the way to speak to a famous detective, but what could he expect from a twin sister who was anything but a twin except for being born on the same occasion?

Shirley was taller than Roger, strong as an ox, ate like a horse, and was healthier than any self-respecting horse ever thought of being. She was that poisonous type of person who romped into the dentist's chair, had her teeth quickly and easily cleaned, and was all through for another carefree six months. Perfect teeth. Not a filling in her head.

"No calls for me?"

"I told you I'd call you if there were. Don't I always?"

"What time is it?"

5

"Roger, what's the matter with you? This is the third time you've asked me."

"I just want to double-check."

"Well, it's nearly four o'clock, and good-bye," said Shirley, and hung up, doubtless to cope with some oven crisis.

Roger took a last look around. He hated to leave his beloved office, but he had to. His phone line ran only as far as the kitchen. Sighing, he dropped down the tree house ladder in his spider-monkey fashion and reentered the outside world.

When he opened the screen door into the kitchen, Shirley was taking a pan of brownies out of the oven. She inspected them with great satisfaction.

"Perfect," she said, and gave him a sharp glance. "No thanks to you." But then, not being one to hold a grudge, she added, "Want to try one?"

"Are you crazy? With my tooth, eat a brownie?"

"Oh, I forgot about that silly tooth of yours," she said with that callousness peculiar to those who have never endured a filling. "Is that what you're so jumpy about?"

"I have to call Doc Butterick at four to see if he can take me today, that's all. Who says I'm jumpy?" snapped Roger, and jumped like a jumping jack as the phone rang. Shirley's ponytail bobbed as she glanced at him.

"Are you ever a bundle of nerves! I certainly hope he takes care of you, so you'll stop running around looking like a scared rabbit. Go see who it is."

7

Affronted by her scared-rabbit comparison, Roger gave her a withering glance that failed to wither her and stalked in to the phone.

"Hello?"

"Hello, is that you, Inspector?" asked a man's voice, but before Roger could reply the connection was broken.

"Hello? Hello?" It could have been Doc, but it also could have been any one of about six other older men he did business with on his egg route. "Hello? . . . Darn the phone company anyway! The service gets worse every day!"

He hung up and fidgeted for a moment, expecting the caller to try again. Then he looked up Doc's number, dialed it, and got a busy signal, which made him hang up in a hurry. Maybe Doc was trying to reach him. Once more he waited. Once more he lost patience and tried the number. Still busy.

Now his hope for a last-minute reprieve began to falter and fade. With his luck, Doc was probably on the phone changing someone else's appointment so he could fit in Roger. And whoever had called was probably someone who wanted to change his egg order for tomorrow.

"Who was it?" asked Shirley.

"I don't know. The line went dead. I'll tell you, the phone company's going to get a hot letter from me!" Roger threatened as he stumped back through the kitchen. Then he thought of still another matter to be irritable about. "Where's Thumbs, anyway? Why hasn't he showed up? He said he was going to come over."

Thumbs Thorndyke was his best friend and one of his two assistants in the egg business, Shirley being the other. One of Roger's many activities involved selling the excess eggs produced at Hessian Run Farm. The farm's owner, Mr. Chadburn, was a millionaire financier who was also a chicken fancier, and because he fancied so many chickens he had more eggs than he knew what to do with until Roger came up with the idea of selling them for him around the village. Roger's egg route had become an East Widmarsh institution. His catchy slogan, "Every egg from a prize chicken," accounted not a little for its success.

"What did you want to see Thumbs about?" asked Shirley.

"Nothing. I just — well, he said he'd be here," complained Roger. Having Thumbs around to talk to would have helped keep his mind off his misery, but even that had been denied him. It was that kind of day. Even Thumbs had let him down.

"I'm going down to Doc's office," he announced gloomily as he headed for the door.

"Have fun," said Shirley, and earned herself another glare.

Even when he was his normal cheerful self, Roger

Tearle did not look it. It so happened he had a face that would make his fortune in a tear-jerking soap opera if he ever decided to become a television actor.

His eyes, his eyebrows, and his mouth all slanted down at their outer corners, giving him the expression of someone who had just lost his best friend. And right now the gloom was real. Leaning forward on his bicycle, all knobby knees and sharp elbows as he raced along, he could have passed for a junior version of the Grim Reaper.

Even when East Widmarsh's lone police cruiser rattled by, driven by its lone policeman, it was all Inspector Tearle could do to summon up a brave smile and raise a hand. Constable Mervin Stubbert returned the greeting, which was more than he would have done a brief time ago, prior to their collaboration on the Milford Arson Case. Before then Constable Stubbert had looked upon Roger as a boy buttinsky and had labeled him the nosiest kid in town, but since the arson caper they had worked in harmony.

The center of the village being located only four blocks from Roger's home, he reached it in almost less time than it takes to tell, and leaned his bike against the side of East Widmarsh's only office building. The village square slept in the sunshine, with hardly a person in sight, nor was the Cramer Building exactly a beehive of activity. Roger spoke to a dog who trotted by and received a tail-wag in reply, and that constituted the whole

of the traffic that was passing through the square at that
hour.

The two-story building he entered was an old-
fashioned piece of architecture with wide corridors and
high ceilings. Dr. Butterick's office was on the second
floor. Standing at the foot of the staircase, Roger discov-
ered his throat had become very dry. A short detour to a
nearby bubbler seemed absolutely essential before he
went any farther.

The corridor was empty and the building silent as a tomb. The dark brown varnished floorboards creaked dolefully beneath his feet as he paced his melancholy way to the bubbler. Wondering why empty hallways in old buildings were so depressing, he gulped water absent-mindedly.

"Ouch!"

That tooth again. It did not take kindly to ice water. Rubbing his lean jaw alongside the throb, he returned to the front of the building and slowly mounted the stairs.

At the top he paused to gaze with hopeless eyes down the long, bare, gloomy corridor. Here it was, the Last Mile, with the Chair at the end, and he didn't even have a chaplain to help him walk it. Grimly, forcing one dragging foot in front of the other, passing the closed doors of one silent office after another, he finally reached the last door on the right, near the rear staircase, a door that bore the dread legend, Amos P. Butterick, D.D.S.

Roger had one last small, unpromising hope left. Maybe the door would be locked. With his heart beating hard, he tried the handle.

Unfortunately it turned.

The small waiting room was empty. The desk behind the waist-high counter on one side of the room was bare except for a telephone off its hook. Obviously Miss Neal, Doc's receptionist, had left for the day. Roger gave the telephone a dark look, then turned his attention to the door of the room Doc worked in. It was closed. Doc was busy. Should he rap on the door and let Doc know he was there? On the other hand, Doc must have someone on the line, which meant he would be coming out to the phone in a moment, so perhaps he should wait.

Even as he was trying to decide, a sound from within made his hair stand on end.

"Mmmmmmmm!"

Roger's throat was suddenly dry again, as dry as if he had never visited the bubbler. Someone with a mouthful of little sponges and clamps and long pointed instruments and dentist's fingers was in there, suffering. Next, Roger supposed, he would have to listen to the nasty whine of the Drill.

"Mmmmmmmmmmmmmmmm!"

Worse and worse! Legs trembling, he rubbed cold, clammy palms on the sides of his shorts. A little of this sort of entertainment went a long way. What was Doc doing to the poor devil? Was he —

"Ulp!"

Now the horrible sound changed to something even more bloodcurdling, something almost like a stifled cry for help. And hearing it, Roger the Fainthearted was suddenly transformed into Inspector Tearle, whose razor-sharp intelligence was ever on the alert to analyze circumstances and put two and two together.

What had occurred to him was this. Whenever Doc had to drill or probe, he never failed to murmur soothing comments and words of encouragement as he worked.

"Don't be worried . . . Just a little more, now . . . E-e-easy does it . . . All be over in a jiffy . . . We're al-l-l-most there . . ."

Yet not once had Doc spoken.

In two firm strides Inspector Tearle had reached the door. And as firmly as he strode, he rapped.

"Doc?"

"Ulp!"

Without further hesitation, he opened the door. And there, bound and gagged in his own chair, sat Amos P. Butterick, D.D.S.

Two

ONE THING was immediately apparent. Except for his feelings, Doc was unhurt.

On the other hand, judging from the fire in his eyes and the blazing complexion of his large, jowly face, he might be carried off by apoplexy if he were not released at once.

Springing forward, Roger gamely attacked the knot in the towel that formed the gag. Doc jerked his head sideways.

"Mmmmmm!" he ordered, and Roger gathered he was referring to his instrument tray. Of course! Good point. No time to be picking at hard knots, and this was a hard one, tied by someone who knew how to tie knots. Inspector Tearle instantly eliminated all women as possible suspects.

There were scissors of a sort on the tray, but they hardly looked suitable for cutting through a towel. The material was not thick, not fuzzy toweling or anything like that, but still . . .

A knifelike instrument seemed to hold more promise. Roger seized it and stepped behind Doc to go to work.

"Mmmmmmmmmmm!" complained Doc, but Roger was quick to reassure him.

"Hold still! This is going to work fine . . . Just a little more now . . . E-e-easy does it . . . There we are!" said Roger as he sawed his way through the last threads and Doc spit out the gag.

"Dammit, Roger, you've ruined my best scalpel!"

"Oh! Sorry!"

"Call the police!"

"Constable Stubbert?"

"No, not that idiot! Call the state police!"

"Yes, sir!" Roger rushed to the door. "What shall I tell them?"

"Tell them — oh, get me out of here, and I'll tell them myself!"

"Yes, sir!" Roger rushed back. He studied Doc's bonds, which seemed to be an endless length of quarter-inch nylon line. "Where did he get all this stuff?"

If it were possible, Doc turned a dangerous shade redder.

"I just bought it for my boat! I was looking it over when that fellow turned up, and he even showed me a special knot he uses for nylon line!"

"He knows his knots, all right. This one's a pip," said Roger, struggling away.

"Cut it!"

"What with? Ever try to cut this stuff, Doc? Don't be worried, we're al-l-l-most there . . ."

Doc was a large, heavyset, elderly man who filled the chair to overflowing, and right now he looked like a fat caterpillar in a cocoon. From waist to ankles, he was firmly attached to the chair by round after round of the line, brought back together and knotted around his ankles. But a knot, even this knot, was meat and drink to Inspector Tearle. He was capable of the kind of controlled, patient effort needed to teach a knot who is boss. He was also an amateur magician, and possessed the manual dexterity that helped so much in such emergencies. As angry as he was, Dr. Butterick had to be impressed by the way Roger managed to worry the complicated knot apart. Or at least he should have been. Unfortunately, however —

"For Pete's sake, Roger, are you going to play with that knot all day?" he roared, mere seconds before his rescuer finally managed to undo it. Even then, he was far from free, for all his thrashing around.

"Please, Doc, hold still!" retorted Inspector Tearle, and there was a steely quality of command in his voice that even an angry man could hardly fail to recognize and respect. Or at any rate, anyone would have thought he could not. But, alas —

"Come on, come on, come on!" Doc ranted impatiently, and continued to thrash around with flagrant disregard for steely qualities in voices. "That young bush face! I'll see him in jail if it's the last thing I —"

"Bush face? You mean, he had a beard?"

"Yes! Did you see him?"

"No."

"But he left just a minute ago!"

"He must have gone down the back stairway as I came up the front," said Roger, his hands flying as he unwrapped turn after turn of the cocoon.

"Dammit, if I ever buy any of this confounded nylon line again — Okay, that does it!" said Doc, kicking free of the last two turns. "Come on, let's find out if anyone saw which way he went!"

Roger knew Doc had been doing some jogging — he bragged about it all the time, man his age and all that — he never expected to see anyone quite as portly run down a hall as fast as he did. With Roger close behind, he pounded down the stairs and burst out of the building like an overweight fighting cock.

The village square looked as if its sunny summer slumber had never been interrupted. All was quiet. The only person in sight was a lean old fellow with a straggly gray mustache and a leathery face under a World War I peaked felt hat. With a slightly rheumatic but recognizably military step, he was crossing the village green in their direction.

"There's Old Sarge!" cried Roger. "Maybe he saw something! Hey, Sarge!"

Old Sarge was a good friend of Roger's who lived out on the Chadburn place and did a little gardening for young Chadburn, as he called his fifty-year-old boss. He saluted genially as he drew near.

"Howdy, Inspector. Hi, Doc. What's going on? You two come running out like a pair o' young Chadburn's chickens with their heads cut off —"

"Sarge!" Doc waved his hands in all directions. "Did you see a young punk with a beard run out of here a minute ago?"

"With a beard, you say?"

"Yes."

Old Sarge nodded. "I did notice he had a beard. Couldn't miss it, for that matter. Big beard. Red beard."

"Which way did he go?"

Old Sarge pointed. "Thataway. Jumped on a bike and took off like a six-day racer."

"A bike?" Roger darted to the side of the building for a look. "That dirty rat! He took *my* bike!"

"Your bike? Why, that's as bad as horse thieving, and we used to string 'em up for that!" said Old Sarge indignantly. "Well, the way he was traveling, you better send out a three-state alarm."

"You're right," said Doc. "We're wasting time. I'll go call the state police this minute."

Back to Doc's office they went, and now they were three, because naturally Old Sarge was the sort of man who stood by a friend in need, especially a friend who had had his transportation stolen. As one of the last of the old horse cavalry men, he considered this the lowest crime in the book.

They listened attentively while Doc phoned a nearby state police barracks.

"That's right, he tied me up in my chair and took off!" Doc was presently explaining. "Young punk I'd never seen before, about six feet two and powerfully built with reddish hair and a bushy beard the same color. He came in with a bad tooth and asked me to help him out. Said he'd pay in advance since he was a stranger, and shoved twenty bucks into my hand. Well, I took a look, and sure enough he had a tooth that needed to be worked on right away. So I excused myself and went out to phone a patient I was expecting, to tell him to hold off till four-thirty.

"Well, I hardly got to the phone when this feller shoved someth·ng in my back and said, 'No, you don't!' At the same time he reached around and banged down the doohickey that breaks the connection and next thing I know I'm getting a dial tone. Well, I didn't know what to think. 'You're not turning me in!' he said. I told him I wasn't trying to turn him in, but he said, 'Don't try to kid me! Get in there and get in that chair.'

"I said, 'That's no gun you've got in my back!' and he said, 'Okay, would you rather I bashed you over the head?' Well, twenty years ago he'd have had a fight on his hands, but I'm not as young as I once was, so I got in the chair. He tied me up and put a gag in my mouth, and then he took off. Luckily my next patient came in and found me a few minutes later, but by then he'd got out of town on a stolen bicycle —"

"A Randall-Simpson English bike," said Roger bitterly.

"A Randall-Simpson English bike, and — Yes, that's what I said, a bike. No, not a motor bike, a plain pump-it-yourself bike. . . . Well, it may sound funny to *you*, Sergeant, but that's what happened," Doc declared with some asperity. "What? No, he didn't rob me. He didn't take anything. He didn't even take back his twenty bucks, come to think of it — but from the way he acted, he must be one of your Most Wanted Men. Anyway, he gave me a bad time, and I want that young punk brought to book!"

Doc supplied a few more details he managed to recall about the young punk — striped sport shirt, tan slacks, wide black belt, canvas shoes — then hung up and blew out a snorty breath.

"Look at me. Trembling like a leaf. Roger, I'm in no

condition to go to work on you now," he declared as regretfully as though he were dispensing bad news. "Do you think you can hold out till morning?"

"Can I? Easy! Don't give it a thought, Doc. Why, I'd forgot I even had a tooth!" Not for the first time Roger was impressed with how much attractive wisdom there was in the old adage "It's an ill wind that blows no man to good."

"Got a bad tooth, Roger?" asked Old Sarge.

"Well, not exactly *bad*, but —"

"Blacksmith used to yank 'em out in our outfit," the old campaigner recalled fondly.

"Well, I'm going to straighten things up around here and then go home," said Doc. "You come back first thing in the morning, Inspector, say about eight-thirty. And thanks for coming in just now. It's a lucky thing for me you did!"

They left Doc fussing with his instruments and went outside. Old Sarge ruminated indignantly.

"Well, I declare I don't know what the world's coming to, when a youngster can't leave his bike parked outside the Cramer Building in broad daylight, and a dentist can't do a day's work without ending up roped and hogtied into his own chair." He treated himself to a much-needed chaw of tobacco from the plug he always carried. "But leastways it's lucky that feller wasn't one of them dope fiends come to steal a batch of Doc's drugs."

"I doubt they'd be interested in his stuff," said Roger.

"I don't think they could take much of a trip on novocaine."

"Guess you're right. I suppose it was medical doctors I was thinking of. Well, Roger, I hope they at least turn up your bike before morning. What'll I tell young Chadburn? Can you borrow another bike for your egg route tomorrow, if you have to?"

"Sure, I'll manage, Sarge."

While they were talking, traffic in the square picked up one hundred per cent. A well-known local rattle interrupted their conversation.

"Here comes Constable Stubbert," said Roger. "We'd better tell him what happened."

"Nothing to lose by it, I suppose," said Old Sarge, though his opinion of the officer's abilities was not high.

Roger stepped off the curb and signaled urgently. The old police car bucked to a stop beside them.

"What's wrong, Inspector?" asked Constable Stubbert, for now even he had come to honor Roger's nickname.

"I was hoping you'd come along, Constable!" said Roger, ever the diplomat. "I want to report a crime — two crimes, in fact. A fellow tied up Doc Butterick in his office, and then stole my bike!"

The officer's eyes, which normally tended to be small and bloodshot, grew large and bloodshot. A crime of these dimensions had not struck East Widmarsh in some little time.

2 5

"What? Tied up Doc? Hurt him?"

"No, he —"

"Rob him?"

"No, he just tied him up and took off — on *my* bike!"

"Hmm! On your bike? He stole *your* bike?" said Constable Stubbert, and despite his new policy of peaceful coexistence with Inspector Tearle he was not above a bit of professional one-upmanship. He patted the cruiser's steering wheel as much to say, "You don't see me going around losing *my* wheels!" Roger chose to overlook this display of petty gloating and went on to give him the details. When he had finished, Constable Stubbert redeemed himself somewhat by making a handsome offer.

"Which way did you say he went, Sarge?"

"Thataway, Merv."

"Well, tell you what, Roger. You jump in back, and we'll take a run over thataway and see if we can find any trace of your bike."

"Why, thanks, Constable!"

"You too, Sarge, if you've a mind to."

"Well, it's going toward the farm, so I might as well," conceded Old Sarge, though Roger knew wild horses could not have held him back even if "thataway" had been in the opposite direction.

As Roger and Old Sarge were piling into the back seat, two cyclists appeared.

"Roger!" called Shirley.

"Hey, Roger!" called Thumbs. "What's going on?"

Roger leaned out the window.

"Some guy stole my bike, and we're going after him! I'll explain later!" With a jerk and a rattle, the forces of the law got moving.

Three

TENSE AND ALERT beside the left-hand window, Inspector Tearle was at his busy best, on the lookout for any clue, however slight. Old Sarge sat within discharge range of the other window, in order to take care of excess tobacco juice. Paunchy and relaxed behind the wheel, Inspector Stubbert aired his opinions.

"I'll bet that feller won't go far on no bike," he declared. "You been on one lately, Sarge? Believe me, if you're not used to them, they can murder you."

While both his listeners were wondering how Merv knew, he continued.

"If he went out this way, I'll bet you he didn't get much farther than Half Mile Hill. By the time he pumped up *that* one, he'd of had enough."

The hill in question fitted its name. It was a gentle slope, but it went on for half a mile, and as Roger knew from long experience, even a conditioned bike rider felt the pull in his leg muscles by the time he reached the top. Thinking about it, he had to admit — privately, of course — that Constable Stubbert's theory was not so stupid, at that. When they started up Half Mile Hill he was doubly vigilant, especially when side roads came along.

Old Sarge glanced out the back window and chuckled. "They're still a-coming."

Far back down the road, but managing to stay in sight of the cruiser, were Thumbs and Shirley, pedaling hard.

"Might know it," snorted Roger, but at the same time he could hardly blame them. He had given them good reason to be curious. He could not spare them so much as a fleeting glance, however. His attention was riveted on the road. And suddenly his vigilance was rewarded.

"Stop!" he cried so suddenly that Merv hit the brake and nearly threw them all out of the car. "I mean, do you mind?" said Roger, amending his order hastily. "I think I saw something."

"For crying out loud, Roger, you like to scared me out of my britches!" complained Merv, but Roger was already out of the cruiser and running back to a side road, a narrow sandy dirt road that meandered across the countryside for a few miles in the direction of another main road. Eagerly he knelt and examined the road's surface. Then he stood up and waved.

"Fresh bike tracks, and they're *my* bike!" he announced. "I'd know my tire tracks anywhere."

Not without some protests from his transmission, Constable Stubbert backed the cruiser to Roger's side and stared down at the tracks. Seeing them, he grinned.

"What did I tell you? He couldn't make the hill!"

"You're right, Constable!" said Roger, though he could think of better reasons for the turn. If you were a wanted man fleeing on a stolen bicycle, it only made sense to get off a main road as soon as possible. He waved to Thumbs and Shirley, who were narrowing the gap while the police car was stopped. Then, longing for the days when cars had running boards, which was exactly what he needed to ride on just then, he made the best of it by leaping into the front seat and then hanging out the window. "Go slow, so I can keep an eye on the tracks!"

"Been smarter if he'd stole a horse," said Old Sarge,

forgetting for the moment that horses did not exactly abound in East Widmarsh. "Nothing like 'em for slipping away into the brush."

The tracks continued, straight ahead, but not for long. In no time at all the car rounded a bend and there in the grass alongside the road lay the getaway bike.

"My bike!" cried Roger in a tone not unlike that a mother might use in crying "My baby!", though of course much more manly.

"What did I tell you?" said Merv, relishing one of his finest moments. "Didn't take me long to find it for you, did it?"

Roger was out of the car again, examining his pride and joy and finding it unharmed. In his excitement he made a professional error.

"Fingerprints!" he groaned, and jerked his hands away, too late. After a booboo like that, committed squarely in front of Constable Stubbert, there was nothing left to do but cover up quickly. "Oh, well, they'd be hard to pick up from rubber grips, anyway. Practically impossible," he declared, without being entirely certain of his ground, and glanced around hurriedly to create a distraction. "The important thing is, where did he go from here?"

Fortunately Constable Stubbert was not the breed of police officer who worried his head much about such details as fingerprints, and therefore missed a golden opportunity to score off Inspector Tearle. As he grunted his way out of the front seat and stared around unenthusiastically at the brambly underbrush that lined both sides of the narrow road, the Constable looked like one of those porky rural police officers so often portrayed in TV melodramas. Constable Stubbert was not about to exert himself beating the bushes for a man who sounded more like a nut than a criminal.

"He could of took off in any direction from here," he declared. "Might even have hitched a ride with some farmer over to Route 12. I'd better go over and report finding your bike to the state boys and let them take it from here. Can you make it home all right, Sarge?"

"Always have, Merv."

"Thanks a lot, Constable," said Roger as the officer slid his paunch back under the steering wheel.

"Any time, Inspector." Constable Stubbert lifted his hand in a patronizing wave, and with a clash of gears the cruiser rattled away down the road.

"Can I make it home!" snorted Old Sarge. "He ought to do as much walking as I do. It would take off some of that pot."

"Hey! You found it!" Pink-faced from their exertions on Half Mile Hill, Thumbs and Shirley appeared round the bend in the road. They braked to a stop beside Roger's bike, and Shirley looked at him accusingly.

"I knew you were up to something, the way you were acting — wanting to see Thumbs and then saying, 'Oh, nothing' when I asked why."

"Well, that's where you're wrong. When I left home, I didn't know anything was going to happen," said Roger, and gave them a quick rundown on what had happened at Doc's office.

"But who was the man? Why did he do such a thing?" asked Shirley, causing Roger to clutch his brow in a manner peculiar to brothers with infuriating sisters, and causing her to suffer from the sort of sarcasm all too familiar to the sisters of infuriating brothers.

"You won't believe it, but I wondered the same things myself. I'll tell you what — when I meet him, I'll ask him!" said Roger, grinning sourly at Thumbs, who responded with a sickish grin. Thumbs Thorndyke had won his nickname by being all thumbs where anything physical was concerned — he was forever pinching his fingers in something, or hitting his funny bone, or skinning his knees — but he was a loyal and trusted lieutenant, and could be counted on when the going was rough.

Before Shirley could think of something suitably sharp in the way of a reply, Roger had turned his attention to more pressing matters. His woebegone face, combined with his sleuthing activities, had once caused Old Sarge to hang yet another nickname on him, Roger the Boy Bloodhound. The way Roger was nosing along the side of the road now brought it to mind. If Roger had started baying, Old Sarge would not have been surprised.

"What are you doing?"

"Looking for footprints. Doc said the man had on

33

canvas shoes, and I'll bet they had ripple soles. In this sandy soil, they ought to show up . . . Here! Here's one! Not a ripple, but anyway a pattern . . ."

The others joined him for a look.

"I'd say that was a fresh print, all right," agreed Old Sarge. "And here's another."

Beyond the second print, grass had spread to the edge of the road for several yards, but beyond the grassy patch Roger found one more print. It angled sharply toward the edge of the road.

"He turned off here!"

They stopped for a look in the direction the print suggested, and exchanged a confirming glance.

"Deer trail," said Old Sarge, and Roger nodded. A tingle ran along his spine. The thrill of the chase, the scent of danger.

"Must go down to the canal," he said.

"It's not far from here," agreed Old Sarge.

"I think I'll have a look."

The game old man might be stiff in the joints, but he was young in heart.

"Let's go!"

"Okay, Shirley, you and Thumbs stay here and guard the bikes —"

"Nobody's going to touch the bikes," said Shirley. "I want to see what happens."

"Now, listen —"

"Besides, there's safety in numbers."

"Well . . ." grumbled Roger, who had never really expected to get away with his suggestion, anyway, "there isn't time to argue. But be quiet!"

Deer trails provided about the only means of getting through the sort of dense, brambly underbrush that flourished in the woods between the road and the old canal, which had been an important waterway a hundred years ago. And even on a well-traveled deer trail, if you were a human being instead of a deer, there was a good deal of stooping and scrambling involved, of ducking under branches in forcing a passage. They had not gone far before Thumbs tripped on a root and crashed into the underbrush about as quietly as a water buffalo breaking out of cover.

Sighing sharply, Roger stopped, turned, and made a number of exasperated motions with his hands that meant — in his mind, at least — "Stop! Stay there! Don't come any farther! Get lost!" With a resigned expression on her face, Shirley was taking a small strip bandage out of her pocket. They had long since learned to keep such things on hand whenever Thumbs was around. Apparently he was bleeding again. Well, at least that would keep them busy for a moment or two. Roger hurried on, with Sarge close behind. He marveled at how the old man kept coming, and how quietly. Once Roger stopped and pointed in silent satisfaction to a bare spot with a clear imprint on it. They were on the right track.

After a few more yards, he could see a glint of water

ahead through the trees. They were nearing the canal. Once he reached the canal bank, the man they were tracking could pick his way along the towpath in either direction without much trouble. But if he went to the left, the canal would take him back toward the village. Unless he had lost his sense of direction, he surely would not go that way. He would turn the other way.

Creeping forward, Roger felt certain he knew now where the trail was going to come out. He remembered a crumbled place on the bank where deer were able to get at the water easily. Edging forward, he peered round a bush and saw he was right.

He also saw something that froze his blood.

Kneeling on the bank was a young man with a big bushy red beard. He was holding his head tilted back with one hand, while with the other he put a glittering sliver of glass to his throat.

Four

Without an instant's hesitation, Inspector Tearle sprang forward.

"Stop!" he cried. "Don't do it!"

The piece of glass went flying as the man's hand jerked, and he stared around wildly at Roger.

"You nitwit," he thundered, "you nearly made me cut my throat!"

Nothing could have deflated Inspector Tearle more quickly.

"I what?"

"You nearly made me cut my throat!"

"But — but I thought you *were!*"

"Were what?"

"Cutting your throat!"

The beard stared at him.

"Now, why would I do a crazy thing like that? I was shaving!"

"*Shaving?*"

"Certainly! Well, anyway, I was trying to. Or anyway I was going to try to," he said, getting further from a shave with every statement. But then he collected himself and glared defensively. "What's the matter, haven't you ever heard of someone shaving with a piece of glass before?"

Behind Roger, Old Sarge chuckled.

"So that's it! I wouldn't want to try it."

The old man took in their surroundings with a thoughtful glance.

"Funny place to come for a shave," he observed. "Don't look much like a barber shop."

"Well, now, what's that to you?" asked the bearded

one with a show of belligerence, and stared at Old Sarge's hat as though he might have seen it before.

"Why did you take my bike?" asked Roger.

"Oh. That was your bike, was it?"

"Yes."

"Well, I had to get out of town quick."

"I know. I was Doc's next patient. Why did you tie him up?"

They were interrupted by a commotion in the brush. Two more youngsters appeared, one of them with a fresh strip bandage on his shin.

"Hey, what is this, a posse?" the stranger snorted, and moved warily in the direction away from the village. "Now, listen, I don't know how you managed to trail me so fast, but don't get the idea you're going to march me back to *that* town." He sounded as if he expected to be lynched there. "I didn't hurt that dentist any. I only tied him up because I didn't want to be picked up and thrown into any jail. I've got a thing about jails. So I'm going my way, and if you're smart, you'll go yours, and — Oooh!"

All at once his face twisted with pain, and he cradled his jaw gingerly in the palm of one hand. Roger could not help feeling a throb of sympathy, right in his own ailing molar.

"Got a bad tooth?" he asked.

"Mmmm," the man mumbled through the beard, and shot an irritable glare Roger's way. "You don't think I'd have gone to the first dentist I could find, right there in

39

town, if it hadn't been driving me nuts, do you? Now beat it, all of you, and leave me alone!"

Broad-shouldered and rugged, he looked about as approachable as a wrought-up grizzly bear and about as stoppable, too. Few more frustrating moments had plagued the action-packed career of Inspector Tearle. A mystery was on the point of walking out of his life unsolved. Such an event was unthinkable. Something had to be done about it, and done quickly.

"Burgessville's the next town," Roger remarked.

"I know," snapped the bearded one over his shoulder.

"By the time you get there, all the dentists' offices will be closed."

The man's pace faltered. Obviously the thought of not reaching a dentist soon was agony to him.

"I'll get hold of one somehow!" he blustered.

Split-second decisions are, of course, something any successful detective often finds himself having to make. Despite his interest in the field of criminology, Roger could hardly claim as yet to know a criminal type when he saw one. The young red-bearded monster confronting them, his face twisted into evil lines by pain, might be someone who had recently bludgeoned six people to death in a remote farmhouse, for all Roger knew. But on the other hand, what Roger did know was that he had showed no tendency to be rough with Doc, and that instead of grabbing Doc's keys and taking his car, he had fled on a bicycle.

Did real desperadoes make their getaways on English bicycles?

And besides that, a touch of toothache made them comrades, as far as Roger was concerned. Looking at that suffering face, he was moved more by the instincts of Florence Nightingale than of Sherlock Holmes.

"Maybe we could help you," he said.

His unexpected words got in under the man's guard. Roger saw him hesitate, and watched sudden, wistful hope well up in the hard blue eyes. "What do you mean, help me?"

"Maybe we could get you to a dentist."

"Huh! Why would you do that?"

There are times when frankness is in order. Roger recognized this as one of those times.

"Because I want to know what this is all about," he said. "If you'll tell us, maybe we can help you. If you're not a crook or something, there's no reason you can't tell us what's going on."

The beard wiggled in understandable amazement. Then the face hardened, though not without noticeable regret.

"Nothing doing. I'm not talking to anybody," he said — and then added a bargainer's postscript. "Not for a while yet, anyway . . ."

Inspector Tearle had all he could do to continue to look his melancholy self. Now they were getting somewhere.

"What do you mean, not for a while yet?"

"Well, I — Well, I don't exactly know yet what's going on myself. I've got to talk to somebody first, and I can't do that till tomorrow." He glanced around in a desperately shifty way.

In the busy mind of Inspector Tearle, possibilities were clicking into place like marbles in a pinball machine.

"You're not here to rob a bank, or anything like that?"

"A bank? In East Widmarsh? What bank?" came through the beard convincingly. "I'm not out to rob anybody. In fact, maybe I'm trying not to *be* robbed," he added in a darkly cryptic mumble.

Inspector Tearle was satisfied. It was decision-making time, chance-taking time, and he was ready.

"Okay," he said, "I'll make a bargain with you. If you'll promise to tell us exactly what's going on, tomorrow, then we'll get you to a dentist, and hide you out till morning."

The bearded mouth fell open, apparently causing a draft of cool air to hit the bad tooth. He winced again, but hope was back in his eyes. Where Inspector Tearle was concerned, there was one thing it was hard not to do. It was hard not to trust him. As a detective, this was one of his greatest assets.

The beard nodded. He had come to a decision.

"Listen, I'll do better than that. Just help me get this tooth taken care of, and I'll sit down with you and tell

you the whole story, even though I'm not sure yet . . .
Well, anyway, it's a deal!"

"Good!"

"So now — how are you going to work it?"

Five

Who was the stranger?

"Call me Marty," he had said when Roger asked him what his name was. "Call me Marty. That'll do for now." But who was he, really?

Once again the posse, as Marty had called it, was picking its way along the deer trail, but this time there was no need for silence. And Old Sarge, for one, was not keeping silent. He was expressing his doubts.

"Roger, I don't mind saying that if you'd been any other youngster your age, I'd have stepped in and put my foot down back there. You're talking about helping a fugitive from justice, and that makes you a whatchamacallit. One of them accessories."

"An accessory after the fact," said Roger, who liked to be precise about such things. He stopped to defend himself.

"I thought about that, Sarge. But if I don't charge him

with stealing my bike, and if Doc doesn't charge him with anything, then the police wouldn't have anything to hold him on, and there wouldn't be any fact to be accessory to, before or after."

"Well, but what made you so sure Doc won't charge him with assault and battery, or some such thing?"

"He wouldn't do that if it was going to get me into trouble."

Old Sarge blazed a nearby tree trunk with tobacco juice and chuckled.

45

"Well, no, I suppose he wouldn't. Well, sir, the rest of your scheme is just harebrained enough to work, I'll admit. Of course, you haven't said where you plan to hide him out —"

"Oh, I'll take care of that when the time comes," said Roger somewhat evasively, and started on again.

"But I'm sure you have a good place in mind," said Old Sarge with a glint in his eye.

"There's always the tree house," said Shirley.

"The tree house?" Thumbs hooted at the idea. "Merv would have a conniption fit if — Ow!" he cried, because he had managed to lift his head at the wrong instant and had smacked his forehead against a low branch.

"Take it easy, Thumbs!" urged Roger. "Listen, Sarge, are you game to let me give you a ride back to town? You can sit on the seat and I'll pump. After all, it's mostly downhill."

"An old gaffer like me on the back end of a bike? Well, I guess I'll have to try it. Beggars can't be choosers."

When they reached the road and walked back to where the bikes lay on the grass, however, Old Sarge eyed them dubiously.

"Hmm. These here critters ain't exactly the kind of mounts I'm used to, Roger. You sure you can manage it? Maybe —"

"Car coming!" announced Thumbs, whose keen sense of hearing was as outstanding as his ears. Old Sarge looked hopeful. The sound became audible to them all, and then recognizable enough to make them grin.

"If I'm any judge of rattles . . ." said Old Sarge, and a moment later Merv confirmed his judgment by coming round the bend doing thirty miles an hour.

But the ancient East Widmarsh cruiser was not alone. Its clatter had masked the presence of a second car which now appeared behind it, a state police patrol car driven by a young officer wearing a hat not unlike Old Sarge's.

Seeing them standing beside the road, Constable Stubbert came to an abrupt stop that nearly caused the first two-police-car pileup in the history of the county.

"You still here, Roger?" Merv's small red eyes darted around, taking in the brush again, and he grinned indulgently. "Hot on the trail, huh? Well, did you find him?"

"Sure, nothing to it," said Roger, snapping his fingers. "We trailed him through the woods, and there he was."

Merv laughed with comfortable disbelief at this bit of boyish bravado.

"Nice work, Inspector!"

Behind him, the state trooper had climbed out of his car with an annoyed look on his serious young face.

"Merv, how about giving someone a little warning when you're going to stop? I darn near creamed you."

"Be alert, fella, be alert," counseled Merv, and waved his hand at Roger. "This is the kid I was telling you about, the one who had his bike stolen, and that's the

47

bike, right where I found it for him. Inspector, this is Trooper Muldoon. We're going to have a talk with Doc."

Trooper Muldoon cast a professional eye around him at the thick underbrush that lined the road. He gave Roger some earnest advice.

"Listen, kid, this guy that took your bike sounds like some kind of nut. If I were you, I wouldn't go fooling around in the woods looking for him. Not that he's likely to be there, anyway. More likely he thumbed a ride over on the highway."

"You're probably right," said Roger. "Anyway, I'm glad you came along." He turned to Merv. "If you're going to Doc's, why don't you take along your star witness?" he suggested, pointing to Old Sarge.

"Why not? He saw the guy come out of the building and take off on the bike," Merv explained to Trooper Muldoon. "How about it, Sarge, want to come along?"

"Why not?" said Old Sarge, echoing Merv.

"We'll follow along on our bikes," said Roger, causing Merv to grin again.

"I figured you would," he declared, and jerked a thumb at Roger as he told the trooper, "The Inspector here is a real eager beaver."

"Well, that's fine," said the serious-minded trooper, "but from now on, leave the job to us, huh, Inspector? If the man hasn't caught himself a ride out of the state, we'll find him."

Old Sarge seemed to be having a choking spell. While Roger pounded him on the back, he spat out his cud of chewing tobacco.

"Thanks, Roger," he gasped. "That durn near went down my Sunday throat."

Thumbs and Shirley did their best not to grin, though their best was none too good. In the meantime, Inspector Tearle's scheming mind had not been idle. He grimaced painfully.

"Ooooh! Doc didn't get a chance to work on my tooth, and it's giving me fits," he said. "Officer, do you happen to have a first-aid kit in your car?"

"Of course!" Trooper Muldoon sounded as if, given the slightest encouragement, he could have quoted word for word the regulation calling for inclusion of first-aid kits in all state police vehicles.

"Well, could you give me a couple of aspirin, or some pain pills? I'd sure appreciate it."

"Why not?" said Trooper Muldoon, picking up the phrase that was going around, and strode off to his car. He was back in a moment carrying an impressive box with a large red cross on its lid.

"I've got some stuff here that's stronger than aspirin, but I'm not sure it's okay for kids to take," he said worriedly as he opened the box.

It was all Roger could do not to draw himself up.

"I'm practically thirteen," he said with icy dignity, "I don't think you have to worry."

The trooper held out a small bottle.

"Can you swallow one of these without water?"

"Sure."

Roger opened the bottle, shook it into his hand, capped the bottle, and handed it back. Putting a tablet to his mouth, he swallowed with a movement of the throat that reminded Old Sarge of a heron gulping down a fish.

"Thanks! That's great!"

"I hope it's not too strong," said Trooper Muldoon, his mind obviously still groping among Rules and Regulations, but Roger reassured him.

"Don't worry, I'll be okay. We'll see you there," said Roger, and while the men were climbing into the cars he made a show of picking up his bike and getting ready to follow them. So did Thumbs and Shirley, but once the cars had pulled away and gone out of sight they were not surprised to see Roger lay his bike down again.

"How many pills did you palm?" asked Shirley.

"Three."

"I knew it!"

"Did you see me do it?" asked Roger, alarmed. As an amateur magician who even owned a wand and a swami turban, it would have hurt his pride to think his hand had not been quicker than the eye.

"No, I couldn't see you do it," said Shirley, "but I figured that was what you were up to. Did you really swallow one?"

"No, I thought I'd better keep it for Marty. You two wait here. I'll be right back."

When they reached Dr. Butterick's pleasant white clapboard colonial house in the village, the two police cars were parked out in front. From egg route force of habit they swerved into the driveway, left their bikes beside the garage, and went to the back door, where Mrs. Butterick let them in.

An energetic, white-haired, motherly woman, every bit as plump as Doc, Mrs. Butterick was noted for the cheerful abundance of her speech. Some folks claimed the only time Doc got a chance to do the talking in his family was when he was cleaning her teeth. On the other hand, she was one of the best cooks in town, and the appetizing smells that filled the kitchen were enough to remind even Roger, preoccupied as he was, that it was getting on toward dinnertime.

"Hello, Shirley, hello, Thumbs, why, Roger, I hardly recognized you without a carton of eggs in your hand," she declared as they entered. "By the way, I'd like two dozen in the morning, I'm having the Handicraft Club here and I want to make one of my angel foods, my goodness, Roger, wasn't that a terrible thing that man did to the Doctor, thank heaven you came in when you did!" she said, all in one breath. "Merv and that young state trooper and Sergeant Maclain, I understand Sergeant Maclain saw the man run out, they're in the parlor talking to the Doctor, I suppose that's why you're here, so why don't you go right on in, and don't forget my extra eggs in the morning."

"We won't, Mrs. Butterick, two dozen," said Shirley, who never forgot order changes, and they walked through the house to the parlor.

"Well, Inspector, I hear Merv located your bike for you," Doc told Roger when he appeared in the doorway. "That's something, anyway. Sit down, kids. I've just been going over what happened for the trooper here."

They sat down on a big sofa next to Old Sarge and looked on while Trooper Muldoon asked precise questions and made precise notes on his report pad. When he had finished, the two police officers departed together. Doc left the room to see them to the door, which gave Old Sarge a chance to nudge Roger in the ribs and say, "Took him some pills, didn't you?"

"Yes."

"I expect he was mightly glad to see them."

"Yes, he was. They ought to hold him till we pick him up."

When Dr. Butterick returned, Roger said, "Doc, we don't want to hold up your supper, but we do have something important to talk to you about."

"Go right ahead, Inspector. We're not in any hurry." Doc jerked his head in the direction of the back of the house and sat down with a sigh. "Mrs. Butterick's on the phone again. If there's a woman left in this town who hasn't heard about what happened, she either isn't home or her line is busy. When it comes to wire services, my wife beats the Associated Press by a country mile."

Roger was happy to have Mrs. Butterick telephoning. If she was talking, she couldn't be listening, and for the moment he preferred to speak to her husband in private.

"The thing is, Doc, when Merv came by just now, it was a break for us, because we were planning to come see you anyway."

"You were? Why?"

If Inspector Tearle had a fault (and he did), if he was sometimes a prey to vanity (and he was), these all too human flaws in his character became apparent at moments such as the present one. His weakness for drama came to the fore. He thoroughly enjoyed any occasion when he could make someone's mouth fall open.

"Well, we wanted to have a talk with you about the man they're looking for," said Roger, "because we just had a talk with *him*."

Doc's mouth did not disappoint him.

"What?" Doc scrambled to his feet. "You know where he is?"

"Yes."

"And you let those two officers sit here and —"

Old Sarge raised a hand to stem the rising tide of indignation.

"Steady, Doc."

"But of all the crazy — ! Are you going to let a criminal —"

"I don't think he really is a criminal."

"Not a criminal? Listen, what do you call —"

"Well, now, look, Doc. What did he really do? He tied you up, but he didn't hurt you. Instead of robbing you, he didn't even take back his twenty bucks. Instead of taking your car keys, he ran out and grabbed my bike. Who ever heard of a hood making his getaway on a bicycle? And then he rode it only a little way, and left it where it would soon be found — which was very foolish on his part, in fact. Now, does all that add up to a hardened criminal?"

The dentist sat down with a grunt.

"Sounds more like a fathead!" he admitted.

"That's right. Well, I don't think he *is* the smartest stranger that ever showed up in East Widmarsh. For that matter, I don't think he's a stranger," added Roger. "He knew where to turn off and find a deer trail over to the canal — I'm sure of that. I think there's somebody in East Widmarsh he wanted to see, and that he found out he couldn't see whoever it is till tomorrow. And he promised if we'd help him, he'd tell us exactly what it's all about as soon as — as — well, as soon as we'd helped him."

Roger's tone had faltered, causing Doc's gaze to sharpen suspiciously.

"What do you mean, help him?"

Inspector Tearle found it necessary to clear his throat. The delicate stage in their two-power talk had been reached. He spread his hands in an appeal.

"Well, as a matter of fact, Doc, he's suffering something awful with that tooth of his, so I promised we'd get him to a dentist."

"Get him to a dentist?" Doc was quick to point out the impracticality of this promise. "At this time of day? Where did you think you'd be able to find him a dentist . . . ?"

Old Sarge was enjoying himself, watching Doc's expression change as the truth about Inspector Tearle's outrageous intentions smote him like a stone.

"Inspector! You're not suggesting that *I* —"

"Well, gee, Doc, what other dentist is safe? You're the only dentist in the whole state the police won't have on the lookout for him!"

"Oh, my sainted aunt! But, *Roger* —"

"What's more, he even paid you in *advance*," Roger reminded him. "And if you could see how he was suffering, Doc . . ."

Poor Dr. Butterick never really had a chance.

Six

SUPPER PROVED TO BE a difficult meal for Roger. Naturally his parents were eager to have his eyewitness report on what had happened. In the course of giving them a carefully edited version of events, he kept forgetting to chew with caution. When he did forget, his ticklish tooth let him know it was still there.

"Doc didn't feel like working on me after what he'd been through, so I have to go back tomorrow morning," he explained.

For once Shirley had the goodness to say very little, bowing to her brother's forcible suggestions on the way home. As Roger had pointed out, the best way to avoid a slip of the tongue is to keep your mouth shut. It was a strain, but on the whole she managed pretty well.

There were questions that took careful handling.

"Where do you think that man went after he ditched your bike, Roger?" asked Mr. Tearle.

57

"Merv figured he might have caught a ride with some farmer."

"Well, yes, he might have. Or, for that matter, he might be hiding right there in the woods."

"We thought of that, of course," nodded Roger.

"I hope you didn't try to track him!" said Mrs. Tearle, instantly alarmed, for she knew how her son the detective operated.

"Well, we did take a look around, but then Merv came back with Trooper Muldoon, and he told me to leave it to them."

"Well, I should hope so! I don't want you out looking for someone as crazy as that, Roger Tearle. Why, he might kill you!"

"I hope they find him," said his father. "He sounds like he ought to be locked up!"

Shortly after eight o'clock, Inspector Tearle and his two assistants were once again pedaling through the streets of East Widmarsh. A soft summer twilight was beginning to fuzz the air, and birds twittered sleepily in the trees as the three bikes swept past. Most of the people they saw along the way were in back yards, lingering around the mellow glow of charcoal grills, and did not notice them go by, for which Roger was glad. By now almost everybody had heard about the incident at Doc's office, and all of them would have wanted to ask questions. At another time Roger would have been glad to oblige, but at the moment they could afford no delays. Time enough for that when they made their rounds in the morning, delivering eggs.

His tooth prodded him with one of its barbed-wire tickles as he remembered his appointment.

"Listen, I'll have to cut out tomorrow morning in time to be at Doc's by eight-thirty," he told the others gloomily. "I guess you can handle the rest of the route without me."

"Sure," said Thumbs. "Tomorrow's not too tough."

"Two dozen extra for Mrs. Butterick, and an extra dozen for Mr. Driscoll," said Shirley, exercising her bookkeeper's mind.

They were prompt, and they were not kept waiting. They had scarcely leaned their bikes against the side of the Cramer Building before a dark green panel truck stuck its nose into the square and made a wide turn around the corner. The truck, one of several belonging to Hessian Run Farm, was used principally to transport the antique furniture Mrs. Chadburn was forever buying at auctions. At the moment, however, the only antique it was transporting was Old Sarge. He swung it to the curb beside them.

"Hop in, kids! Guess we better have one of you in back."

"I'll ride in back," said Thumbs, and while he was opening one of the rear doors to climb in, Roger and Shirley joined Old Sarge in the front seat.

The old campaigner was in high spirits.

"Well, this is one time I don't mind driving one of these danged contraptions. Ordinarily I don't take kindly to machines. After all, it was machines that mechanized the cavalry, and ruined it. But tonight, I don't mind admitting, this beats a horse. One thing you can't do is hide a man in a horse. The last ones that did that were those Greek fellers at Troy. I expect you know that story, Roger? I always figgered them Trojans weren't too smart, falling for a trick like that. Hmp! Drag a wooden horse jammed full o' soldiers into the middle of East Widmarsh, and see how far you'd git!"

On the edge of town, beside the canal, a numerous family named Plummington lived in an old stone building that was once a mill. East Widmarsh's squatters, some people called them. About a hundred yards past their place a dirt road, hardly more than a trail, ran in through the woods to the canal. Old Sarge backed the truck into the dirt road. Roger and Thumbs got out and posted themselves beside the rear doors, ready to swing them open the instant Marty appeared.

They waited. Roger scanned the woods with impatient eyes, and whistled cautiously. He hoped all the Plummington kids were in bed by now, or at least in the house, but he doubted it.

When there was no response to his whistle, he went to the front of the truck for an anxious consultation.

"Darn it, the least that crazy guy could do is be here

6 0

on time! You don't suppose something happened to him, or he decided to take off?"

"Oh, I don't see why he'd do that," said Old Sarge. "And what could happen to him around here, less'n he fell in the canal?"

"You even synchronized your watches," Shirley pointed out. "Maybe his watch is running slow."

"Well, I don't like this waiting around," complained Roger, who never did like waiting around, for that matter. "I'd better walk in and see if I can find him."

"Go ahead. We'll hold the fort."

By now, under the trees that arched the trail, gathering darkness provided a melancholy gloom that matched Roger's thoughts. He was sorry now he had not insisted on hearing Marty's story before lifting a finger to help him. But Marty had been so miserable with that tooth of his that he had scarcely been able to concentrate on what he was saying, and had certainly not felt like talking, even if he had been willing to. And Roger had been too sympathetic to press him. Had that been a softhearted mistake unworthy of a dedicated detective? If, after all the effort Roger had gone to, the ungrateful rascal vanished without a trace, and Roger had to spend the rest of his days suffering torments of unrelieved curiosity, wondering what this unsolved case had been all about, life would be grim indeed.

Under the circumstances, it was not surprising that he forgot himself so much as to grit his teeth, and paid for it with a sharp tickle that almost made him exclaim aloud. His spirits sank to a new low for the day. That cursed ticklish tooth of his! If it hadn't been for that, he wouldn't have felt so sympathetic. He would have been sterner, and driven a harder bargain.

His frame of mind left him totally unprepared for the sight that greeted him when he reached the canal. For a second or two he could only stare unbelievingly. For there, lounging on one elbow, taking his ease on the bank like some Sunday idler without a care in the world, sprawled Marty.

"Hey, Marty!"

The sharp undertone in which Roger spoke would have made a nervous man leap like a trout, but Marty merely glanced around at him and smiled pleasantly.

"Oh, hi, Roger."

"What are you doing here? We're waiting for you!"

"You are?" Marty lifted his wrist and gave his watch a vague look. "Gee, I'm sorry. I guess I lost track of the time."

"How long have you been sitting out here in plain sight?" asked Roger, horrified, while his eyes flew around in six directions. "Listen, there's about a dozen kids living a hundred yards from here, and they run around in the woods and up and down the canal all the time. Any one of them is likely to see you here. Come on, let's get going!"

"Yes, sir! Lead the way," said Marty, chuckling. Nobody could have been more agreeable as he got to his feet. "It's mighty nice of you to go to all this trouble, Roger. And believe me, I appreciated those pills. They really helped," he declared as he ambled along behind Roger like an amiable trained bear.

His leader glanced back, alarmed.

"You didn't take all three at once, I hope?"

"No," said Marty. "Not all at once. I spaced them out."

"Oh. Well . . . still . . . well, never mind, let's get a move on!"

Roger rushed forward as they neared the end of the road.

"Quick, Thumbs! Get the doors open!"

He turned and gestured sharply to the stroller behind him.

"Hurry! In here!"

"Well, hello! Nice to see you again!" said Marty, patting in the general area of Thumbs' shoulder, but missing it. "Okay, in we go!"

And as Roger and Thumbs took his brawny arms, expecting to help him step up to enter, he fooled them by sort of melting forward and climbing in on his hands and knees. Thumbs' eyes were round.

"What's with him?"

"He took those pills, and they really relaxed him."

"Gee, you can say that again! Well, he looks harmless, but —"

"You sit up in front with us," said Roger. "It's a short ride."

"I think I will," said Thumbs.

They shut the doors and went forward.

"All set?" asked Old Sarge.

"Well, yes and no. Anyway, he's in," said Roger. "We decided to give him plenty of room, so move over, Shirley."

They jammed into the front seat and Roger explained further during the brief return trip. Back at the Cramer Building they found Doc's car parked outside. They pulled up behind it and took a look around. A couple of cars drove past on the other side of the square. Otherwise, nobody was in sight. When they opened the back of the truck, Marty seemed to be dozing.

"Hey, Marty! Come on! We're here!"

"Mmmmm? So soon?"

Not without some strenuous tugging and hauling did they manage to get him outside and onto his rubbery legs. Propping him up among them, they hustled him into the building. Marty chuckled.

"Roger, did you ever feel like a balloon floating in space?"

"Just keep floating," said Roger grimly. "Up the stairs now, and please, pick up your feet!"

"What feet?" Marty inquired pleasantly.

Though it was nearly dark now, there was still light enough coming through the windows to let them see their way up the stairs and along the corridor to Doc's office. Light streamed out as Roger opened the door, and Doc greeted them from his inner lair.

"Well! Come in, and shut that door."

Doc was all business, a man in a hurry.

"Well, young feller, you'd better have a good story to tell when we're through here," he told Marty. "Get in the chair. Sooner we get the job done, the better."

"Yes, sir! I just want to say, you're a kind man to do this, Doc, and —"

"Never mind that, just sit down."

The inner door closed behind Doc and Marty. Inspector Tearle turned to his assistants.

"Go back downstairs and keep an eye out, in case anyone comes around."

In a way, he envied them as they left. A dentist's waiting room was not the sort of place where he cared to linger. Old Sarge sat down and picked up a magazine, but for Roger no magazine would have been capable of holding his attention just then, especially when, in due time, the whine of the Drill assaulted his ears and chilled his blood. His own ticklish tooth twinged sympathetically, and thoughts of tomorrow darkened his mind. At last, however, he could hear Doc say, "Well, that just about does it."

"Sounds like he's finished, Sarge," he muttered, and relaxed with a vicarious sensation of relief.

The pleasant feeling was short-lived. His nerves twanged like bowstrings as light footsteps pattered up the corridor outside. Before he could do more than spring to his feet, the door was flung open.

Shirley burst in and spoke two dreadful words.

"Merv's coming!"

Seven

HIT BETWEEN THE EYES with such a message as this, it is small wonder Inspector Tearle reeled backward and wrestled for an instant with paralyzing panic. But then he recovered himself. And when he did, he spent no precious moments on such time wasters as, "What shall we do?" or "Alas! All is lost!" Instead he whirled and went into action. For the second time that day he let himself into Doc's inner sanctum.

"Doc! Merv's coming!"

It is in such crises that a private detective shows his mettle. A run-of-the-mill sleuth would have had his client climb out the window onto the fire escape to hide, or some such piece of foolishness, leaving all the rest of them standing around in awkward attitudes well calculated to arouse Merv's suspicions. The moment called for the simple stroke of genius, and Roger produced it. As

Marty got slowly to his feet, Roger pointed to a screen that stood in one corner of the room.

"Quick, Marty, get behind that screen!" he ordered — and sat down in the chair himself.

An instant before, Doc had looked flustered. Now his jowly face relaxed, and he grinned. As for Marty, he was as obedient as a robot. He disappeared behind the screen without a word and could be heard sitting down heavily on the floor. Footsteps were clumping up the stairs now at the end of the hall, but before they reached the office Doc had a towel clipped around Roger's neck and was saying, "Open wide! . . ."

Outside in the waiting room, Old Sarge nodded to Merv as the constable poked his head in.

"Evening, Merv."

"Hi, Sarge. What's going on? I saw lights on up here and figured I'd better check, because —"

"Doc's taking care of Roger's tooth. Couldn't do it this afternoon, you know."

"Evening, Merv," Doc called through the open door. "Anything new?"

"You bet there is." Followed by Thumbs, the constable entered the waiting room. He stepped across to the inner door and looked in at Roger. "Give him the works, Doc!" he urged, a hearty chuckle rumbling up from his paunch. "Well, sir, it may interest all of you to know I been doing a little police work, checking around, and I turned up something."

Roger, still opened wide for Doc, rolled his eyes at Merv and said, "Aaahgh?"

"That's right," said Merv. "One of the Plummington kids stopped me a few minutes ago. Said he'd seen a feller with a red beard sitting on the canal bank not a stone's throw from their house."

"Aaahgh?"

"Yep. So maybe our man hasn't gone very far after all."

Roger could feel tiny beads of sweat on his forehead, and was glad he was in the dentist chair, where nervous perspiration looked normal. If Marty started moving around now! . . .

"I got some of the state boys on their way over," continued Merv. "We're going to surround the area and take a look along that stretch of the canal."

"Aaahgh!"

"So just relax, Inspector, and we'll take it from here."

"That's fine, Merv," said Doc, and inserted a drill into its holder. "Now, everybody outside. Roger doesn't like an audience when he's being worked on."

"Okay, Doc, I got to be going anyway. The state boys ought to be here any minute. Enjoy yourself, Roger!"

"Aaahgh!"

Poised in the chair, Roger listened tensely while the constable stopped for a word with Old Sarge.

"What you doing here, Sarge? Doc running a night clinic?"

"No, I had to mosey into town on an errand, so I just come up here to see how Roger was making out."

"I reckon he'll live. Well, see you all later," said Merv, and Roger relaxed as he heard the outer door close behind the departing officer.

"Boy! That was a close one. Okay, Marty, you can come out now. As soon as we're sure that —"

He sat forward in the chair to get up, and as he did he became conscious for the first time of a massive tingle in the side of his face. When he touched his jaw, it felt like a block of wood.

"Doc! Did you —"

"I sure did," said Doc. "I gave you the needle and you were so busy listening to Merv you never even knew it. You ought to bring him along every time."

"But — but —"

"Well, I couldn't just fool around while Merv was standing there watching, I had to make it look good, and besides, this way I can sleep later tomorrow morning. There's too many policemen outside for you to leave just yet, anyway, so —"

"But, D-Doc —"

"Sit back and —"

"But —"

"Open wide!"

"Aaahgh!"

For a few minutes both of them forgot about Marty.

Then, from behind the screen, came a gentle snore. Doc stepped over to take a look.

"By George, he's sound asleep. Well, I don't wonder. He's had a big day, that young feller, and he probably had a good deal of pain from that tooth, too." He returned to work. "Well, let's get on with it, Inspector. Just a little more now. E-e-easy does it . . . We're al-l-l-most there . . ."

And sure enough, in another mere eternity or two the drilling was finished, the filling was in, and Roger was at last able to take that step so thrilling to all mankind, that step that takes one out of the dentist chair.

"Thanks, Doc! Now I'll sleep better, too!" he admitted. He would have liked to spend a few minutes simply savoring his new-found freedom from fear, but the pressure of events ruled out mere personal pleasures. There was too much to do. He hurried over to where Marty sat dozing on the floor and shook his shoulder. "Come on, Marty, wake up! Time to go!"

Marty stirred, sighed, and dropped off to sleep again. Doc came over and said, "Come on, let's get him on his feet."

Together they managed to haul him erect, and by the time he was standing up Marty's eyes had opened, though not wide.

"Wha'?" he asked drowsily.

"My gosh, you'd think that trooper gave me sleeping

pills instead of pain-killers, the way he's acting," said Roger.

"What pills are you talking about?"

Roger explained. Doc looked alarmed.

"And he took three of those bombs? Do you remember the name on the bottle?"

"I think so." Roger made a stab at repeating it. Doc looked less alarmed.

"Oh. Not so bad. He can take that all right. But the combination of that and the novocaine . . . Roger, for a while you're going to have a zombie on your hands. He's going to sleep for about twenty-four hours."

"What? But, Doc, I want to talk to him! I've got to find out —"

"Not tonight, you won't. I may be wrong, but I think you'll have to wait. Come on, I'll help you get him downstairs. Shirley, why don't you and Thumbs go down first and see if the coast is clear?"

Doc turned back to Roger and jerked his head at the young Rip Van Winkle they were holding up between them.

"By the way, just what do you plan to do with him now?"

"Yes, what about that, Roger? I been wondering about that myself," said Old Sarge, fixing Roger with a glittering gaze.

Inspector Tearle became shifty of eye and froggy of

throat. He had been uncomfortably aware of the way Old Sarge had waited him out on this subject, never bringing it up till now.

"Well, Sarge, I thought maybe . . . well, you've got that extra room in your cottage with a cot in it, and you're off by yourself where nobody bothers you . . ."

The old campaigner whinnied dryly.

"You know, I had a feeling you had something like that in mind, Roger," he said. "The feeling come over me strong, from the very beginning."

By now Roger's face had an unusual amount of color in it.

"Well, gee, Sarge, I hope you don't —"

Old Sarge's whinny exploded into a guffaw, and he

gave his scheming young friend a hearty slap on the shoulder.

"Roger, I got the cot all made up and ready," he said. "And from the looks of him, it's just as well!"

With four of them jammed into the front seat and one snoozing on the floor in back surrounded by three bicycles, the panel truck approached the private back road that led across the north meadow of Hessian Run Farm.

The road across was the same one they used every morning when they rode out on their bikes to pick up their eggs. After crossing the meadow, the road curved between two big barns, and the rest of the buildings came into view.

On one side was the henhouse with its wire-fenced enclosure that had figured so importantly in one of Inspector Tearle's major triumphs, the Chadburn Goose Case. Across the road from the henhouse was the cottage occupied by the tenant farmer, Zoltan Dubrovnic, and his family. Up ahead stood the big, rambling colonial farmhouse where the Chadburns lived.

In between were tennis courts, a swimming pool, and the vegetable and flower gardens Old Sarge tended with occasional interference from Mrs. Chadburn. Off to one side was the small prefabricated cottage Old Sarge referred to as his barracks. Secluded amid a grove of big trees, it made an ideal hideaway.

There were lights on in Zoltan's cottage and in the big

74

house, but fortunately nobody was outside to wonder why they were riding out to the farm with Old Sarge at that hour of the night.

It took some rough shaking to rouse Marty when they stopped outside Old Sarge's place.

"Doc's right. We've got a zombie on our hands," groaned Roger as they all helped him stagger inside. Roger and Old Sarge took him into the tiny spare room and helped him out of enough of his clothes to make him comfortable.

"Mmmmm! Bed!" Marty mumbled happily, and tumbled into the cot that provided the room's simple sleeping accommodations. He seemed to fall asleep on the way down. Old Sarge spread a light blanket over him, and they returned to the living room where Shirley and Thumbs were waiting. Roger sighed heavily, a prey to brooding doubts.

"What a mess! Sarge, I shouldn't have got you into this," he said, feeling very guilty. "If you get into any trouble because of this, I'll never forgive myself!"

"What kind of trouble, Roger?" Old Sarge inquired mildly.

"Well, here you are, hiding out a fellow the police are looking for this very minute, and now, instead of finding out why he came to East Widmarsh and what he's up to, we still don't know the first thing about him! Maybe I'm wrong. Maybe he *is* a criminal! For all we know, he could be a homicidal maniac!"

Old Sarge opened the door of the spare bedroom and squinted in.

"The way he's sleeping, I don't think I'll have to lay awake worrying about it," he reported. "Even if he is a homicidal maniac, he won't be working at his trade tonight."

"Well, maybe not, but I still don't like it," complained Roger. "The longer he's here, the more danger there is someone will find out he's here. And if Merv got tipped off, we'd be in a mess. He'd have state troopers over here in no time, surrounding the place."

"Don't you worry about that. Nobody's going to come nosing around," said Old Sarge with totally unwarranted confidence, because he had scarcely spoken when Thumbs, who had been lifting their bikes out of the truck, hurried inside with a warning.

"Someone's coming!"

Now they could all hear footsteps outside. Thumbs peered out into the dark, and whispered another bulletin.

"Uncle Willie!"

Old Sarge nodded. Uncle Willie was a crony of Sarge's who lived nearby in the village and sneaked over for a game of cribbage whenever he could get away from his wife Mabel.

"I'll handle him," muttered Old Sarge, and walked to the door. "Well, evening, Willie. Mabel let you loose, did she?"

"Evening, Sarge. I seen my chance, and I took it!" declared Uncle Willie gleefully, and shuffled inside. He was a small, peppery man much afflicted with rheumatism, and one reason he loved to come over to Old Sarge's was that they generally took something for his rheumatism in the way of liquid refreshment while they were playing their cribbage.

Once inside, Uncle Willie paused to look understandably surprised at finding the cottage full of youngsters at that hour of the night.

"Well, you got a houseful, Sarge! I suppose you're working overtime, Inspector, trying to get on the trail of that feller that tied up Doc in his office. I hear tell you're the one that found him. He must of been a sight, trussed up in that chair," said Uncle Willie with a heartless cackle. "Merv's out looking for that feller, too, I hear, along with some state troopers. Must be some kind of nut, that feller. Hear he had a beard. Mabel was on the phone with Agnes Butterick for quite a spell. Wonder where the feller got to?"

"No telling," said Old Sarge. "Well, Roger, I'm glad you kids came by, and I'll see you in the morning."

"Right, Sarge. Take care."

"Don't worry. I'll manage," said the old campaigner, and they said good night and filed out, leaving him with the tricky business of dealing with Uncle Willie.

"Oh, boy!" muttered Roger as they walked their bikes out to the driveway. "I hope Sarge can keep Uncle Willie's nose out of that spare room!"

77

"What if Marty snores?" said Shirley, and they all groaned. From the cottage came the sound of a radio being turned on good and loud. Roger grinned feebly.

"I guess Sarge has decided he's in the mood for some music tonight. I hope it works!"

As they pedaled home through the darkness on the familiar back road, Inspector Tearle's spirits were once again at low ebb. Was he just a meddler who should have minded his own business? First he had involved Doc Butterick in his crazy scheme, and now he had let Old Sarge in for a lot of grief. And for what? For all he knew, they might be shielding a real criminal!

Sensing his friend's depression, Thumbs tried to point out the bright side.

"Well, things could be worse, Roger. At least you don't have to go to the dentist tomorrow."

It was a point well taken. Roger brightened a little. He had almost forgotten. His ticklish tooth was behind him!

"Say, that's right!" This consoling thought made him realize his normal appetite had been restored. "You know what, Shirl? I can't chew on my left side till tomorrow, but if I'm careful, there's no reason I can't eat a couple of your brownies when we get home."

"No, you can't," said Shirley, "they're all gone."

Roger was in bed, trying to read, when his parents came home from a bridge game and looked in on him.

"How's the tooth doing?" asked his mother.

Here was one of those situations that so often trouble a detective when he has a client to protect. Inspector Tearle got around it by sticking to the truth, but leaving out some of the details.

"Well, I got a surprise tonight. Doc was in his office after supper, and I went up to talk to him, and the next thing I knew he had me in the chair and was filling my tooth!"

"You mean, it's all taken care of?" asked his father. "Well, that's fine. You must feel better about life."

"I do."

"I'm glad you're home," said his mother. "We heard the state police are out looking for that man along the canal."

"Oh?"

Roger gave them his well-considered opinion.

"They're wasting their time," he said.

Eight

Early the next morning Thumbs Thorndyke showed up as usual and the three of them set out for the farm on their bikes to pick up the eggs Zoltan Dubrovnic would be getting ready. When they reached the barnyard, Zoltan appeared in the doorway of the henhouse and gave them his usual glum greeting in his customary broken English.

"Eggs not ready yet."

"Okay, we'll say hello to Sarge," said Roger. Shirley called out the number of cartons they would be needing for the day's deliveries, and they kept going.

Old Sarge was in the vegetable garden, cutting asparagus. He looked like a man who had been under a certain strain.

"How did it go, Sarge?"

"Well, it was a long evening, but I managed. Willie objected to the radio, but I told him I wanted to see if there was any news about that feller they were looking for. Glad I did, too, because once or twice Marty did some snoring. Good thing Willie's hearing ain't any better than it is, that's all I can say."

"Any sign of life from Marty?"

"Not yet. He's still out like a light."

"Do you think he's okay?"

"Sleeping like a baby."

Roger sighed. Even though he had expected it, this was disappointing news.

"Well, we'll check back again after we've made our rounds. Anybody else come nosing around?"

"Not so far."

They went back and sat in the grass alongside the barnyard, waiting for Zoltan and his fat wife Zaza to finish boxing the eggs. Needless to say, Inspector Tearle's mind was not idle.

"Okay, even if we can't find out anything from Marty yet, maybe we can pick up something while we're making our deliveries," he said. "What brought Marty to East Widmarsh, anyway? He must have come to see somebody. If he did, and that person has heard about what happened at Doc's office —"

"*Everybody's* heard that by now," said Shirley.

"Right. So then somebody is going to guess it was Marty who tied up Doc. Which brings up an interesting point. So far as we know, that somebody didn't report anything to the police."

"So that means whoever it is must be a friend of Marty's."

"Well, maybe yes, and maybe no. Because now we come to another interesting point. Why did Marty tie up Doc and run for cover? Judging from what he said, it had something to do with not wanting to be picked up by the police and thrown into jail. He said, 'I've got a thing about jails.' Does that mean he's been in jail before?"

"Gee, I hope not," said Thumbs, suddenly worried. "If he turns out to be a jailbird, we could be in real trouble."

Roger nodded abstractedly, his mind still grappling with the scanty facts at its disposal.

"*Why* did he get so excited at Doc's, though? Let's take it step by step. He walks into the office. Doc is looking over some new quarter-inch nylon line he's just bought. Marty tells him he's got a tooth bothering him, and Doc says he'll take a look at it. But before Marty gets in the chair he looks at Doc's new line and even shows him a special knot he knows. Now, what does that tell us?"

"Maybe he's done some sailing?"

"Well, yes, maybe, but something more important than that. It tells us that, up to this point, Marty is not a nervous guy expecting to be arrested. A nervous guy wouldn't stop to show somebody a knot."

"That's true," said Thumbs. "He'd jump right in the chair."

"He hands Doc twenty dollars in advance, without

being asked, which shows he doesn't have any intention of running out on Doc without paying after he's finished. So far he seems like a nice guy and a square shooter. What makes him change? Well, let's take it step by step. He gets in the chair. Doc takes a look and sees what has to be done. But before he starts to work, he excuses himself and goes out to the phone. He calls me to tell me not to come in till later."

Roger's eyes were blank now, staring into space, as he tried to put himself in Doc's office and see everything that happened, just as it happened.

"I answer the phone, and he says, 'Hello, is that you, Inspector?' and before I can say anything the phone goes dead. Marty has followed Doc to the phone, and Marty has broken the connection. That's all Doc says, just, 'Hello, is that you, Inspec—' "

Roger's mouth remained open in the middle of a word. He had the dazzled look of a detective upon whom a great light had just dawned.

"Inspector!" he repeated, and sprang to his feet, staring down at his assistants. "Do you suppose Marty thought Doc was calling a — a *police* inspector?"

"That's it!" gasped Thumbs. "That's got to be it!"

The excitement of deduction sent Inspector Tearle pacing back and forth on the grass as new questions filled his mind.

"Yes, but why would he suspect Doc of calling the police?"

They all gave this problem their frowning consideration.

"Well," said Thumbs, "he must have been suspicious the minute Doc went out to the phone, or he wouldn't have got up out of the chair and followed him."

"He was ready to be suspicious of everybody," said Shirley. "He couldn't trust anybody."

"He thought somebody had tipped off Doc to be on the lookout for him," suggested Thumbs.

"Somebody who knew he had a bad tooth and might decide to stop at a dentist's," Shirley added eagerly.

Inspector Tearle nodded his approval of all this.

"Good, good. Now you're both thinking," he declared, paying his assistants one of his rare compliments.

"That may be exactly what he thought. But as we know, the truth was that nobody had tipped off Doc about anything. Marty must have thought somebody might report him to the police for some reason or other, but so far as we know, nobody did. But the thing I'd like to know is, what was that reason?"

Roger flopped down on the grass again. Deduction could take him no further. And now a new worry began to nag at him. A Marty who woke up with no ticklish tooth plaguing him might think differently than the ailing Marty who struck a bargain with him yesterday. He might have second thoughts about sticking around and telling his story. He might wake up and quietly take off while Old Sarge was out working in the garden, and never be seen again. Tortured by the thought, Roger stirred restlessly.

"Listen, we've got to keep our eyes and ears open this morning. That's all we can do," he said. "Everybody's going to be asking us questions about yesterday. Maybe someone will say something that will tell us something."

And suddenly he was in a frenzy to get going, jumping to his feet and stalking toward the henhouse.

"Darn it, haven't they got those eggs ready *yet?* . . ."

Their first stop was at a cottage that had figured in one of Inspector Tearle's early minor triumphs, the Grimshaw Campstool Case. Through the use of good, sound deduction, he had recovered a missing campstool for

Miss Grimshaw, and had stood high in her books ever since.

A sharp-nosed spinster, Miss Grimshaw had lived next door to Uncle Willie Jones for sixty years and feuded with him for forty of those years, during which time they had not spoken, though she remained on good terms with his wife Mabel.

"I wish we didn't have to stop at Miss Grimshaw's today," said Roger. "She'll want to ask a million questions."

"Well, so will everyone else," said Thumbs. "It's going to be a slow trip."

"Tell you what, you take her eggs in to her this morning."

"Okay, but you'll never get away with it," predicted Thumbs, and he was right. As usual, Miss Grimshaw was keeping a gimlet eye out her window — "Nosy old fool never misses a thing that goes on!" Uncle Willie was inclined to fume — and she had her kitchen door open before Thumbs was halfway up the back walk.

"Roger, come in here a minute. I want to hear about yesterday."

Suppressing a sigh, Roger kicked his bike stand into position and followed Thumbs up the walk. After a flurry of all the inevitable questions had been answered, Miss Grimshaw said, "Young feller had a beard, they say. What color was it?"

"Sort of reddish, Doc says."

"Reddish, eh? What size was he?"

"Tall, with big broad shoulders."

"They haven't any idea what became of him, I suppose?"

"Not so far as I know."

"You're sure about that?"

"Yes. Why? Did you think you saw him?"

"No, no, nothing like that," said Miss Grimshaw, shaking her head sharply. "Just wanted to know what to look for, in case I *did* see him."

"I don't think you need to worry about that," said Roger.

Their next stop was next door, and there it was Uncle Willie who was waiting for them. In fact, he waylaid them outside his woodshed, before they got to the house, so that he could talk to them without his wife Mabel hearing him.

"Roger, you got any idea what's eating Sarge?"

"Why, no, Uncle Willie," said Roger warily. "What do you mean?"

"Well, he wasn't himself last night, wasn't himself at all," complained Uncle Willie. "Kept his fool radio going all evening, was jumpy as a cat, couldn't concentrate on his cards — I beat him two out of three games, and that's unusual. I'm going to keep an eye on him. I don't think he's well."

"Oh, now, I wouldn't worry about him, Uncle Willie, we saw him just now and he's fine this morning. Maybe it was something he ate," said Roger in what he hoped was his most reassuring tone. All they needed was Uncle Willie nosing around over at Sarge's!

"Well, I don't know. I may mosey over there after a while and see for myself, if I can get away from *her*," grumbled Uncle Willie, jerking a thumb over his shoulder at the house.

"Well," said Roger when they were pedaling on to their next stop, "let's hope he doesn't catch Sarge napping."

"Let's hope he doesn't catch *Marty* napping," said Shirley.

Progress along the rest of their route was as slow as they had expected it to be, but there was nothing unusual or suspicious about any of the questions people asked Roger, nothing that indicated any special interest in the identity of the bearded stranger. By the time they reached the Driscoll place, near the end of their day's route, Inspector Tearle was growing discouraged, and impatient to finish up and get back to Sarge's.

The old Driscoll place, to be sure, was one of their most important stops, not so much because of the eggs they sold there at present, but because of the enormous number they expected to be selling there in the future.

The Driscoll farm was really outside the village proper. Besides the house, there was a large barn, and seventy-five to a hundred acres of pasture land Miss Sophia Driscoll had always rented to a local farmer. Hessian soldiers had once bivouacked in the Driscoll fields during the American Revolution, and even in those days Driscolls had lived there.

Now that Miss Sophia had died, her nephew Cedric stood to inherit the place, and he planned to turn the big, rambling house into a gourmet restaurant, a country inn offering French cuisine. And he was considering having Roger supply him with all his eggs.

Mr. Chadburn, who drooled at the prospect of a good French restaurant in his immediate vicinity, had already agreed to raise the additional chickens required to supply Cedric's needs. And Roger, as the middleman, stood to profit handsomely if only the deal went through. Not only Roger, for that matter, but Shirley and Thumbs as well. All three of them were building their college funds with the money they made from their egg deliveries. Cedric's restaurant, if it worked out, could make quite a difference to those funds.

When Roger and his assistants arrived, Cedric was just coming out of the house, heading for his car. Cedric Driscoll was a big man, dark-haired and clean-shaven except for a small black mustache. Normally he was pleasant enough in a slightly overbearing way, but today he looked nervous and irritable. There was a large bruise on the left side of his heavy jaw. He gave them a brusque greeting, and jerked his head toward the house.

"Give them to Clara. She's in the kitchen. Did you

bring me that extra dozen, Roger? I have a recipe I want to experiment with."

"Yes, we've got it," said Roger, and received a curt nod of thanks. Cedric plunged into his car and drove away. Roger unstrapped the boxes of eggs remaining in his wire basket, took two boxes, and carried them to the kitchen door. Clara Gumper was waiting for him.

Roger had always liked old Clara Gumper. She was a simple soul, a countrywoman, seldom seen in anything but a cotton housedress, usually with an apron over it. She was a thin wisp of a woman with an angular face and a set of false teeth whose whiteness had always reminded Roger of china eggs. She had worked for Miss Sophia for more than forty years, and according to reports her employer had left her enough money to be comfortable on. Cedric had done his best to persuade her to stay on and help him get his restaurant started because Clara was a wonderful cook. But the word was that Clara was determined to retire and go live in Burgessville with her sister.

Whenever Clara Gumper became excited or concerned about anything, she took off her steel-rimmed spectacles and started polishing them with a corner of her apron. She was polishing them now as she stood at the back door, looking worried, but Roger was not surprised. Like everybody else in East Widmarsh, he had heard about Clara having to rush over to Burgessville the day before, because her sister had been taken to the hospital.

"Morning, Roger."

"Morning, Mrs. Gumper. I heard about your sister. I hope she's going to be all right?"

"What? Oh — why, yes, she's fine," said Clara. "It was all a false alarm. Wasn't a heart attack at all, just a little indigestion."

"Oh, that's good. I'm glad to hear it."

"Thank you, Roger. Well, I imagine we'll just be wanting our usual one dozen next time."

"Right," said Roger, and headed for his bike as she turned away from the door.

He was halfway back to the driveway, where Thumbs and Shirley were waiting, before the warning bells began to ring in his mind.

What was going on here?

Clara Gumper was looking worried, and yet she said her sister was doing fine.

Unlike everyone else along the way that morning, Clara had not asked a single question about yesterday's excitement.

But who was Clara's cousin and close friend in the village? None other than Miss Grimshaw — and come to think of it, Miss Grimshaw had asked some pretty particular questions about the bearded stranger, though at the time Roger had not thought much about it. He had been off guard. After all, who would expect to hit pay dirt at the very first place on his route? But now he wondered. Had Miss Grimshaw been asking questions on behalf of Clara?

And then, when you added the fact that Cedric Driscoll had looked nervous and gloomy, and had that dark bruise on his jaw . . . and the fact that Clara Gumper had been unexpectedly called out of town yesterday . . .

"What's the matter, Roger?" asked Shirley, for he had stopped in his tracks like someone who had suddenly been hypnotized.

Roger stared at them blankly for a moment, and then snapped out of it.

"You go ahead and finish up. I'll catch up with you," he said. "I want to talk to Clara for a minute."

And with that he turned and walked quickly back toward the house.

Nine

"CAN I TALK TO YOU for a minute, Mrs. Gumper?"

Clara Gumper was no actress. When she saw it was Roger, back again, she looked more upset than ever.

"What about?" she asked warily.

Inspector Tearle sidled past her into the kitchen.

"It's about what happened at Doc Butterick's office yesterday."

Off came the steel-rimmed glasses, and the pale old eyes concentrated on the corner of her apron.

"Oh. Well, I don't know anything about that, Roger, I was over in Burgessville at the hospital all day."

"I know that, but I just thought . . . well, the thing is, the man who tied up Doc must have come here to East Widmarsh to see somebody, and I'm trying to find out who it was."

"Well, I wouldn't have any idea."

"The police are still looking for him."

"Yes, I heard they were. But he must have got away by now."

Roger shook his head.

"No, he hasn't."

Clara gasped.

"You mean, the police have caught him?"

Again Roger shook his head.

"Mrs. Gumper, can you keep a secret?"

"A s-secret? Why — why —"

"I mean, can I trust you to keep a secret? Because I'd get in a lot of trouble if you didn't."

Clara blinked.

"Why, you know you can trust *me*, Roger," she said almost resentfully. "I would never —"

"Sure, I know you wouldn't. Well, then. He's safe and sound, and I know where he is, and I'm trying to help him."

Clara Gumper dropped her spare frame into a kitchen chair and gaped up at Roger.

"Oh, do you mean it? The poor boy is — is —"

"Yes, he's all right," said Roger, and told her exactly what had happened. Clara hung on every word.

"So he's still asleep, and I still don't know who he is or why he came here. But I don't think he's a criminal —"

"Oh, he's not!"

"Good. Then you do know Marty."

Clara nodded.

"Yes, I do. But his name isn't Marty. It's Matty.

94

Matty Driscoll, and he's Miss Sophia's nephew, or grandnephew, I should say. Like Cedric. Him and Cedric are cousins."

"Well! I didn't know Miss Sophia had any relatives left except Mr. Cedric . . . Wait a minute!"

All at once Roger was recalling an incident from his childhood, nearly two years ago, when he was barely eleven years old and just starting his egg route. He was remembering a morning when he delivered eggs at this same house and found both Miss Sophia and Clara Gumper in tears. Miss Sophia had just got the news, as nearest of kin, that her grandnephew Matty was missing and presumed lost.

"But wasn't Matty killed in Vietnam?" he asked.

"That's what we thought," said Clara. "But now it turns out he was captured and kept in a prison camp for ever so long, and then when he finally got free just a little while ago there was a mix-up with another Driscoll and he didn't even get reported right. I tell you, when he called up here a few days ago and I answered the phone and he said who it was, I all but dropped over in a faint!"

"But you believed it was him?"

"Yes. I wouldn't have known his voice, now that he's older, but everything he said made sense — and he knew me right away, and called me by name, before I even said who it was."

"But you haven't seen him yet, so why did you think he was the one who tied up Doc?"

"Well, for one thing, when I asked how he was, he said he was fine except for a tooth that was bothering him, and maybe he'd have to go to a dentist. And then later he told me he had a red beard. He laughed and said he didn't want it to scare me when I saw him. So when I heard a young man with a red beard had tied up Doc —"

"I see. And you didn't tell Mr. Cedric that Matty had called?"

"I should say not!"

"And it was you Matty came here to see?"

"Yes. When he telephoned, he wasn't sure just when he could come, but as it turned out he came the very next day. And then that turned out to be the very day I had to go over to Burgessville —"

"So then he came here yesterday expecting to see you, and you weren't here."

"That's right. But if you ask me, I think Cedric *was* here," said Clara darkly.

"You do? Why?"

Clara was polishing her glasses again.

"Well . . . well, I think he was here and they had a fight, that's what I think! Cedric says he fell and hit his jaw against the edge of a table, but I don't believe it. You can bet them two would fight if they saw each other because they never got along at all when they were boys and used to come here summers. Matty was the little one then, and Cedric used to bully him something terrible. Miss Sophia and I had to get after him all the time. And if Matty showed up with a beard . . . well! I can just imagine how that would sit with Cedric. If there's anything he hates, it's beards. Every time he sees some young feller wearing one, he comes home mad."

"Well, then, maybe that *is* it," agreed Roger. "Maybe they did have a fight. For one thing, it must have been quite a shock to Mr. Cedric to have a cousin he thought was dead suddenly walk in. I mean, he figured he was the sole heir to this place, and —"

"That's right. Miss Sophia's will is being settled in that court where they take wills —"

"Probate court," said Roger, drawing on an extensive legal background gained from the reading of countless Perry Mason stories.

"In fact, that was the main reason Matty was coming to see me," Clara added significantly.

"What do you mean?"

"Well, not long before Miss Sophia died, she called me up to her room one night and had me witness a paper she'd written out in her own hand. And if you ask me, it was a new will."

"You didn't read it?"

"Certainly not!" said Clara, affronted by the very suggestion. "Wasn't none of my business what it was. All I had to do was sign as a witness to her signature, and I did. But it was what she said that made me think . . ."

"What did she say?"

"Well, she said, 'This may never be needed, but I'd

never forgive myself if it was and I hadn't taken care of it.' Now, I know she never quite gave up hope that maybe Matty hadn't been killed after all. How could she, poor thing? They were the only two she had left in the whole world, him and Cedric. Cedric's folks were killed years ago in an airplane crash, and Matty's folks both died young — his mother just five years ago this fall. Anyway, putting two and two together, that's what made me think it was a new will."

"Did you tell Matty about it?"

"No, I didn't want to mention a thing like that over the telephone. I just said I had something important to tell him."

"I see. Well, all this still doesn't explain why he thought Doc was getting the police after him, though it does explain why he 'has a thing about jails,' as he put it. As soon as we finish our deliveries, we'll go back out to Sarge's and see if he's awake yet. And as soon as I can, I'll work out a way for you and Matty to get together. So for now, just sit tight. And try not to look so upset. Either that or tell Mr. Cedric you've had news your sister's worse again, so he won't wonder about you."

Nothing was more exhilarating to Inspector Tearle than a session of successful sleuthing. As he hopped on his bike and set out to catch up with Thumbs and Shirley, he could not have been more pleased with himself.

He had pedaled along briskly for a good two blocks before the personal consequences of what he was doing suddenly hit him like a blunt instrument. He stopped pedaling abruptly, and coasted along looking like a cyclist who had turned into a statue. It was a good thing there was no traffic, because he might not have seen it.

What if Matty inherited the old Driscoll place instead of Cedric? Or what if the whole business was tied up for years now in the courts?

What would happen to Cedric's restaurant?

And what would happen to the biggest egg deal of Roger's career?

Even if Cedric still ended up inheriting the place, he would probably be so mad at Roger for helping Matty that he wouldn't give him his egg business after all. Any way Roger looked at it, he saw himself as a loser. And not only himself, but Thumbs and Shirley as well. Thanks to his meddling, they would lose out, too.

At that moment, as though Fate were determined to rub it in, Cedric passed in his car, returning home. He may well have wondered why Roger gave him such a feeble wave, and did so with such a hangdog look.

It was a miserable, guilt-ridden Inspector Tearle who rejoined his assistants as they were making their final delivery of the morning.

"What's the matter?" asked Shirley. "No luck?"

Roger smiled bitterly.

"Plenty," he said, "if you want to call it that."

He told them everything he had learned, and they were duly impressed by the brilliance of his deductions and the sharpness of his interrogation, but their compliments were just so much salt in his wounds.

"Yes, yes, it's all very fine, but don't you see where it's going to leave *us?*" he said, and pointed out the disastrous effect events were bound to have on their own fortunes.

"I've done it this time," he declared, punishing himself. "I've really put us in the soup up to *here*."

Thumbs and Shirley looked at each other for a moment, and then it was Shirley who took a good look at things and produced some much-needed common sense.

"Now, listen, Roger, don't be a jerk. Even if we'd never found Marty —"

"Matty."

"Well, Matty, then — even if we'd never found him, he wouldn't have just disappeared. All of this would have come out sooner or later, anyway."

"Yes, but if I hadn't got us involved, then Cedric wouldn't have any reason to be mad at us."

"So what? What's the difference? There won't be any restaurant now, anyway. If Matty and Cedric hate each other, you can bet Matty's not going to let Cedric have the farm without a fight. He's just as much Miss Sophia's grandnephew as Cedric is."

Roger eyed his sister glumly, but behind the glumness there was gratitude. She had succeeded in easing his sense of guilt and making him feel a little better. Still . . .

"Wouldn't it be great if Matty turned out to be an impostor?" he muttered wistfully. "Listen, maybe he is! Maybe he's some GI who knew the real Matty and got the idea of impersonating him . . ."

But even as he spoke, the notion sounded more and more like a bad TV story. And he could see it sounded the same way to the others. He sighed sadly.

"Well, never mind. We won't get anywhere standing around here. Let's go see if Matty's awake yet, and take it from there!"

When they reached Hessian Run Farm, Old Sarge was nowhere in sight. As they approached his cottage they could hear the spattering sound of water running in a shower. Sarge appeared at the door.

"He's up! I got him into the shower and told him to stay there till it wakes him up if it takes all day."

He was surprised at the quiet reception his news got.

"What's the matter, Roger? I thought you'd be pretty excited."

"A lot's happened, Sarge," said Roger. "Wait'll you hear."

When they filed inside, Matty turned off the shower and called, "Was that the kids?"

"Yep."

"Good! I'll be right out."

Sarge glanced at Roger.

"You find out something?"

"Yes."

"Is he —"

"I think he's all right, but we'll see."

Old Sarge went out to the kitchen, from which a violent smell of coffee was circulating. While he was gone, Matty came out of the bathroom, tucking the last of his shirttail into his pants. He looked a good deal better than he had the last time they had seen him.

"Wow! I feel like a new man! Hi, everybody!"

"Hi, Matty," said Roger, and watched his mouth fall open in the midst of the red beard.

"Hey! How do you know —"

"I've been having a talk with Clara Gumper."

Without taking his eyes off Roger, Matty sat down in a chair.

"Roger, you're really something else. How did you find out she had anything to do with me?"

Roger told him. He told him everything he had learned. While he was talking, Old Sarge came back and silently handed Matty a mug of coffee. Matty took a sip, and his eyes opened wider than ever. Old Sarge's cavalry brew was strong enough to wake up the dead, let alone someone who was only supposed to be dead.

When Roger had finished, Matty said, "Well, all I can say is, you didn't leave me much to tell."

"I wouldn't say that," declared Roger. "We still don't know what really happened between you and Mr. Cedric, or why you tied up Doc and went tearing off on my bike."

"Well, yes, that's true. I guess there are a few little loose ends left," admitted Matty. "Okay, I'll tell you. First off, Clara was right. We did get into a fight. What happened was, I got to the house, and who should come to the door but this guy with a nasty little black mustache, the kind that always sets my teeth on edge. I knew right away it had to be Cedric. It was just what I would have expected of him.

"Well, I walked in and introduced myself, and he nearly flipped his wig. At first he wouldn't believe it, but then somehow he knew it was me. Who else would he hate that much on sight? So then he said, well, he didn't know why I had showed up, but I might as well know right away that Aunt Sophia had left him the farm and he was going to start a French restaurant.

" 'A French restaurant?' I said, and the idea was so ridiculous I had to laugh. Well, when I laughed, Cedric went wild. He started for me, and I said, 'Hold on, I've got a bad tooth!' because I couldn't stand the thought of that tooth being jolted. But Cedric kept coming, so there was nothing to do but cream him first. So I did."

"You knocked him down?"

"And out. Or almost, anyway. I guess he hadn't really taken in the fact I'd grown a lot since we were kids, and wasn't someone he could push around any more. But anyhow, I decided right away I'd better get out of there before he came to and started anything more, because hitting him had jarred my tooth almost as bad as getting hit would have, and it was really jumping out of my head. So I took off and started walking back toward the center of town, and by the time I got there I knew I couldn't stand the pain much longer. Well, I remembered there used to be a dentist in the Cramer Building, old Doc Thompson, so I went over to see if he was still there. He wasn't, but Doc Butterick was listed, so I went up to see him.

"By now I was beginning to wonder if Cedric would get the police after me. I didn't think he really would, but then I'd no more than sat down in the chair when Doc excused himself and went out to the telephone. It seemed suspicious, him doing that, so I followed him out, just in time to hear him say, 'Is that you, Inspector?' Well, I guess it was a crazy thing to do, but that set me off, because I've got this thing about jails, any jail, after what I went through. Can't stand the thought of them."

Roger shook his head sadly.

"Well, I hate to tell you, Matty, but Doc was calling me, and he was only calling to change my appointment. That's my nickname — Inspector."

At first Matty just stared. Then he slapped a hand to his forehead.

"Don't tell me! You're the — the inspector . . . ?"

"Yes."

"You mean, all I had to do was sit there in the chair and get my tooth fixed, and nothing would have happened?"

"I'm afraid so."

"Oh, boy. Why do I always jump the gun?" For a moment Matty held his head. Then he shrugged. "Well, what's done is done. The question now is, where do I go from here?"

His square jaw set, and he looked like someone who could be very stubborn.

"I'll tell you one thing, whether there's a new will or not, I'm not going to let Cedric just walk off with that farm! Not on your life! Walk off with it and turn it into a French restaurant? After I've been dreaming all my life about what *I'd* like to do with it?"

"What would you do with it?" asked Roger.

"I'd turn it into a horse farm!"

Old Sarge sat straight up in his chair.

"What?"

"All my life the one thing I've wanted to do is raise horses — and that's the place I could do it."

Needless to say, this statement was music to the ears of an old cavalryman.

"By Jo, I knew you had the right stuff in you!" he declared. "Why, the old Driscoll place would be ideal fer —"

"A horse farm?" said Roger absently, and his naturally melancholy face remained as melancholy as ever. But anyone who knew him well might have suspected that the glint in his eye represented a sudden ray of hope. Ideas were coming now, thick and fast. He stood up.

"Well, listen, if there is a new will, like Clara thinks, then I'll bet I know who has it."

"Who?"

"Mr. Arkwright."

"That old lawyer? Is *he* still going? My gosh, he must be a hundred years old!"

"Nothing like it," snorted Old Sarge, with an old man's touchiness about age. "I doubt he's even touched eighty yet."

"Well, anyway," said Roger, "he was Miss Sophia's lawyer, and . . . he'll be in his office in the Cramer Building, so . . . Wait right here!"

Ten

HALF AN HOUR or so later, Cedric Driscoll was staring out the kitchen windows with a harried expression, watching for Mr. Arkwright's car and wondering why the old lawyer wanted to see him.

When a vehicle turned into the driveway and stopped, however, it was not the one he expected. It was a truck from Hessian Run Farm, with Old Sarge at the wheel and Thumbs and Shirley at his side. They did not get out, but seemed to be waiting.

"Now, what the devil do they want?" Cedric wondered irritably. "Something about eggs, I suppose."

Clara, who was cleaning the stove, turned to peer out.

"Yes, here comes Roger," added Cedric, as Inspector Tearle swerved his bike into the driveway. "I guess they were waiting for him. Well, they'll have to wait some more, because here comes old Arkwright."

Some distance behind Roger — Mr. Arkwright was a cautious driver — came the old but well-kept sedan of the family lawyer. Mr. Arkwright stopped behind the truck. He stepped out of his car. Old Sarge and the youngsters climbed out of the truck. Old Sarge and Roger opened the rear doors of the truck. And while Cedric's eyes nearly popped out of his head, his cousin Matty climbed out of the back end of the truck.

"Mr. Arkwright, this is Matty Driscoll," said Roger. The two men shook hands, but before either could say anything the kitchen door of the house seemed to explode open.

Beet-red with anger, Cedric glared at them from the doorway and bawled, "What's going on here?"

Mr. Arkwright raised a courtroom hand.

"Now, Cedric, let's conduct our business inside in an orderly manner," he said as he led the way firmly toward the house. "I hear you two had a scuffle yesterday. We don't want any more of that."

Clara Gumper brushed past Cedric and rushed outside with a glad cry.

"Oh, it's Matty! It *is* Matty!"

Matty hugged her and led her back inside, following the others into the house while Cedric stood away from the door, fuming.

"What's this all about, anyway? Who arranged all this?"

Mr. Arkwright nodded in Roger's direction, causing Cedric to look as if Roger had stabbed him in the back.

"This young man," said the lawyer. "Shortly before I telephoned you, he brought me the amazing news that Matthew Driscoll was alive and here in East Widmarsh. That being the case, and because of certain other — ahem — circumstances which Roger explained to me, it seemed expedient to hold this meeting as soon as possible. Now, if we may go into the parlor and sit down . . ."

In Mr. Arkwright's world, interested parties sat down for the reading of wills.

They all filed obediently into the parlor and sat down, Matty and Cedric as far across the room from each other as possible. Roger watched Cedric's face as the lawyer, in measured tones, explained about the new will Miss Sophia had written out and left in his keeping, to be used if by some miracle Matty proved to have survived.

"To call it a new will is perhaps an exaggeration," said the lawyer. "Actually, it is more a codicil to her existing will — but a most important one. Miss Sophia never gave up hope, and now we see that her hope was justified."

Roger had been thinking a lot about Miss Sophia, and he knew she had always been one to do the fair thing. If she had done so now, then perhaps. . . . He watched the lawyer take out a paper, unfold it, and clear his throat. He began to read the brief document.

It left the farm to be divided equally between Matty and Cedric.

Miss Sophia had been exactly as fair as Roger had hoped she would be. He breathed a sigh of relief. And while he did so, Cedric sagged in his chair, pale and wan and defeated, a man whose dream had been shattered. His eyes roamed the room despairingly, and fell on Roger. The sight of Inspector Tearle seemed to give him some cold comfort.

"Well, Roger, I hope you're satisfied," he declared. "Now there won't be any restaurant, because I haven't the money to buy him out, even if he'd sell. So you've just blown the biggest egg contract you'll ever see!"

The moment had come. It was now or never, strike while the iron was hot. Roger stood up, nervous but determined.

"I don't see why," he said. "You want to turn this place into a restaurant. Matty wants to make it a horse farm —"

"A horse farm?" Cedric flared up at the mere notion of such a thing. "Over my dead body —"

"But why not?" persisted Roger. "He doesn't need the house to raise horses in, and you don't need the barn and pasture to feed your guests in . . ."

A sudden silence fell on the room as Roger's remarks sank in. He turned and gazed out the window.

"Just think how nice it will be for people eating in here

to look out and see beautiful horses running around in the pasture . . ."

Cedric's thunderstruck eyes flicked back and forth between Roger and Matty.

"Roger!" he cried. "Are you trying to make us . . . *partners?*"

"Why not? Think how pleased your Aunt Sophia would be!"

"But — but —"

"Oh, Cedric!" Clara Gumper's face was glowing. "If you'll do that, if you two will make up, I'll stay on and help you! I'll work my fingers to the bone, I'll —"

"Of course, the first thing Matty will have to do," Roger continued persuasively, "is to shave off his beard, if he's going to stay around here."

"What?" cried Matty. "Now, wait a minute —"

"Well, if a young guy with a red beard showed up in town right now, Merv and those state troopers would grab him in a minute."

"But —"

"Anyway, you were trying to shave it off the first time I saw you," Roger reminded him, "so why should you mind doing it now?"

Meanwhile, Cedric was getting some of his color back. And now Roger's latest suggestion seemed to affect him like a tonic. He brightened visibly, even though he still glowered at his cousin.

"Well . . . if he'd get rid of that crummy beard," he allowed in a gruff voice, "Maybe I could stand to have him around . . ."

Matty glowered back at him.

"Well . . . if he'd shave off that foul little mustache . . ."

Matty stroked his crummy beard, Cedric fingered his foul little mustache, and for a moment they continued to glower. Then somebody snickered — it might even have been Inspector Tearle — and, for the first time, the cousins grinned feebly at each other.

Minutes later three bicycles were on their way to the village square. Never one to leave loose ends around at the conclusion of a case, Inspector Tearle was on his way to Doc Butterick's office. It was important for Doc to be briefed on the latest developments, so that he would not let anything slip.

Furthermore, Doc would make an especially good audience, and Inspector Tearle never minded a good audience.

Their timing was fortunate. When they arrived, Doc was closing up to go home to lunch.

"Come in, come in!" he said, opening up again for his three visitors. "I'm glad you came by, Roger, because I want to check your new filling, anyway. I want to make sure it's smooth and the bite is good."

Roger gave him the whole story, with minor interruptions from Shirley, and then sat down in the chair for his checkup.

"Well, I'm glad you brought me up to date, Inspector," said Doc, as he thrust his little long-handled mirror into Roger's mouth and took a look. "If I happen to meet Matty somewhere out in public, I'll act as if I never saw him before. . . . Hmm. Filling looks fine. Now, Roger, I didn't want to bother you last night, when you had so much else on your mind, but while I was doing that big filling I noticed another cavity we ought to take care of, before you wind up with another ticklish tooth. Just a small one — you won't even need novocaine. So while you're here, what say we get it out of the way?"

"What? But —"

"E-easy does it, now. Just sit back —"

"B-but, D-Doc —"

"And open wide!"

"Aaahgh!"